## CAST OF CHARACTERS

FAMILY
SECRETS

*Five extraordinary siblings. One dangerous past.
Unlimited potential.*

**Faith Martin**—The renowned epidemiologist is in a race against time to cure an outbreak in a small mountain town, but can she stay immune to the dashing local doc?

**Luke Winston**—Will the town physician and widowed single dad give Faith the family she's always wanted?

**Jake Ingram**—He's remembering the past, but could the little girl who cries for help in his dreams be *the* Dr. Faith Martin, and one of his missing, genetically engineered siblings?

**Agnes Payne and Oliver Grimble**—Jake Ingram has foiled all of the scientists' plots to kidnap the Extraordinary Five. But this time the evil duo has a foolproof plan....

## About the Author

## LINDA WINSTEAD JONES

is an award-winning author who's been writing
romantic suspense, fantasy and historical romance
novels since 1994. *Fever* is her fortieth book, and
she was able to combine many of the elements she
loves into the story. There is a touch of fantasy in
*Fever*, as well as intrigue, family drama and, of
course, romance.

"Normally it's the hero who saves the day, but
Faith is an extraordinary heroine in an extraordinary
situation," Linda says. "She's dedicated her life to
saving others, making small and large sacrifices
along the way. No matter what her gender, that's the
mark of a true hero. Watching Faith and Luke fall in
love in the midst of a crisis was a roller-coaster ride,
one I thoroughly enjoyed."

Linda invites you to visit her Web site at
www.lindawinsteadjones.com.

# FEVER

## LINDA
## WINSTEAD JONES

*Silhouette Books*

Published by Silhouette Books

**America's Publisher of Contemporary Romance**

Special thanks and acknowledgment are given to Linda Winstead Jones for her contribution to the FAMILY SECRETS series.

**SILHOUETTE BOOKS**

ISBN 0-373-61375-X

FEVER

Visit us at www.silhouettefamilysecrets.com

**Printed in U.S.A.**

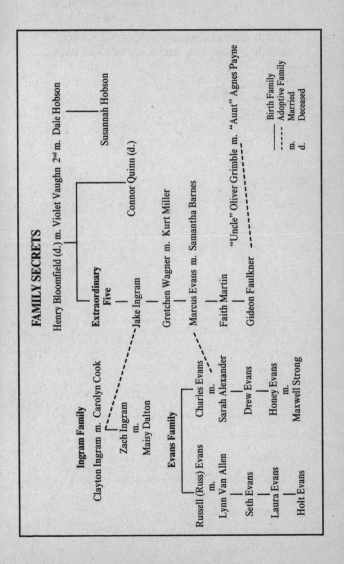

# FAMILY SECRETS

Henry Bloomfield (d.) m. Violet Vaughn 2nd m. Dale Hobson

Susannah Hobson

**Extraordinary Five**

Jake Ingram

Connor Quinn (d.)

Gretchen Wagner m. Kurt Miller

Marcus Evans m. Samantha Barnes

Faith Martin

Gideon Faulkner

"Uncle" Oliver Grimble m. "Aunt" Agnes Payne

**Ingram Family**

Clayton Ingram m. Carolyn Cook

Zach Ingram
m.
Maisy Dalton

**Evans Family**

Charles Evans
m.
Sarah Alexander

Russell (Russ) Evans
m.
Lynn Van Allen

Drew Evans

Seth Evans

Honey Evans
m.
Maxwell Strong

Laura Evans

Holt Evans

———— Birth Family
------ Adoptive Family
m.      Married
d.       Deceased

With a special thanks to Virginia Kantra,
who is a great lady and a joy to work with.

# Prologue

Jake Ingram leafed through the papers in the opened folder on his desk, then returned his attention to the computer screen. It was good to be home, if only for a few days, but he couldn't take his mind off what still needed to be done. No one could continue to live at this hectic pace and not be affected in a negative way. Still, when he tried to clear his mind and relax, even for a few moments, he found it impossible.

His meeting with Matt Tynan and Samuel Hatch hadn't made the tasks he had taken on any easier. The search for Agnes Payne and Oliver Grimble, Coalition scientists who had been involved in the original Bloomfield experiments, was not progressing well. If they could locate Payne and Grimble they'd likely find former CIA agent Willard Croft and Gideon, Jake's own brother, with them. Hatch had been looking for Croft for twenty years, and had stumbled across his share of leads. But without help, Hatch's hands had been tied. Croft always managed to slip through his fingers.

Years ago, Croft had covered Payne and Grimble's tracks with a house fire in which they were supposedly killed. Gideon had been assumed lost with them, but all that time they'd been in hiding. All those years spent shaping Gideon's genius...

Jake dropped his head into his hands and closed his

eyes. He had to learn to focus on one impossible mission at a time. Right now his top priority had to be finding Faith. His sister was out there, somewhere, not knowing who she was or what dangers awaited her. If the Coalition found her first, if they triggered her hypnotic hypersuggestibility, what might she be able to do? Genetically engineered to be a diagnostician and a medical wizard, she could be used in frightening ways, particularly in this day and age of biological weapons.

Despite all their efforts, Faith hadn't been located at any major hospital in the U.S. Searching wasn't an easy task. Faith's name might have been changed at the time of their hypnosis, as Grace's had been changed to Gretchen and Mark's to Marcus. Then again, that might not be the case. Memories that had been returning slowly teased the corners of his mind. Ten years old, her structured world being torn apart, Faith had become hysterical when Mark had been ripped away from her and drugged before her eyes. It was possible that by the time they'd calmed her down, time had become a problem. There was also the issue of individual resistance to take into account. Faith had been small, he remembered. Quiet. But she had also been very stubborn.

Jake shoved his paperwork aside. Faith could be anywhere. Anywhere in the world. They didn't even know without question that she was a doctor!

The phone rang, and Jake answered quickly. "Ingram."

"Hi. It's Marcus."

Jake relaxed a little. "Aren't you supposed to be on your honeymoon, little brother?"

"We're back in Delmonico," Marcus said. "Since

I've been away from the phone for a few days, I wanted to call and check in.'' He hesitated. ''Have you had any luck locating Faith?''

Jake could almost hear his brother holding his breath as he awaited the answer. ''No,'' he said gently.

''You have to find her,'' Marcus said. He was frustrated, as they all were. ''We can't let the Coalition get their hands on Faith.''

''I know. We're doing all we can. I promise you that.''

''Let me help. I can take leave if you need me.''

Jake sighed. At this point, there wasn't much more they could do. Gretchen was heading the search, directing the investigation from the island of Brunhia, and she was doing everything humanly possible to find her little sister. ''You know I'll call if there's anything you can do.''

''I hate feeling helpless.''

Jake understood, too well.

''I'm remembering things,'' Marcus said, his voice lowered slightly.

As they all were. ''Me, too.''

''Bits and pieces, mostly, but the memories are so real. Sometimes it's like everything I forgot for so long happened yesterday. Faith was…she wasn't strong. Smart, yes, but…I'm not saying she was weak, but she wasn't strong. Right?''

''Fragile.'' Jake supplied the word Marcus was looking for.

''Yeah, that's it,'' Marcus said. ''Fragile.''

''Next to you, *I'm* fragile,'' Jake said with a rare smile.

''You know what I mean,'' Marcus said. ''Faith needs someone to look out for her.''

"Yeah." Jake's smile faded. As children, Mark and Faith had looked out for each other. He was strong and she was not. She was brilliant and he…well, Mark had often had trouble understanding things the others took for granted. Faith guided Mark and Mark shielded Faith. Jake silently cursed the people and the circumstances that had torn them all apart.

"I'll call you the minute I hear anything," Jake said.

Tara walked into the room, her eyes hardening when she eyed the phone in his hand. They had mended a few fences, temporarily at least, but an awkward tension remained between them. Even so, she expected his undivided attention now that he was home, and he couldn't give it to her.

One of these days he was going to have to tell Tara everything. Because they were engaged to be married, she deserved to know the truth about who he was, where he had come from and what he still had to do. He just hadn't been able to bring himself to say the words he knew she wouldn't understand.

Tara seemed not to be aware of the new, tightened security that surrounded her. She was under surveillance at all times, just as Jake was, in case the Coalition tried to kidnap or harm them, but she had no idea. Jake, on the other hand, was very aware of the change in his everyday life. He didn't like the situation, but at this point there was nothing he could do.

"I thought maybe we could have a late dinner tonight," Tara said, a tight smile blooming as Jake ended the call with Marcus and turned his attention to her.

"Could we make it early?" Jake asked. "I have a meeting this evening."

Tara's forced smile died, and she pursed her lips, pouting. "I can't make an early dinner. My mother's planning a party for her friend Edith, remember? I told you about it. I promised I'd help. We're interviewing a new caterer late this afternoon. Can't you cancel your meeting? Or reschedule it?"

He shouldn't be angry with Tara for asking him to cancel his meeting so she could interview a caterer; she didn't know what was going on in his world, and until he sat her down and explained everything, she wouldn't. Since she had no idea how much his life had changed, he shouldn't be annoyed with her for being, well, Tara. Still, he sounded snappish when he said, "No."

She waved a disgusted hand in his direction. "Fine. Maybe tomorrow."

Jake knew he should go after Tara as she stalked out of the room. He could smooth things over with a few words, as he had last time they'd argued. But he stayed put as the front door slammed behind his angry fiancée.

# One

When she was out of the country for extended periods of time, it was the grocery store Faith missed most. Such simple pleasures. Pushing a cart up and down aisle after aisle, shelves laden with every kind of food imaginable. The temperature in the building was constant, and mindless music played softly over the intercom. The entire experience was utterly soothing.

She threw a second bag of cookies onto the growing pile of goodies in her cart.

"More cookies?" Janine asked with a wry grin. "It must be nice, to never have to worry about your weight." She sighed as she looked Faith up and down. "It's just not fair."

Faith smiled at her roommate. Janine had been on a diet since they'd met six years ago, and before, to hear the woman tell it. Not that Janine needed to diet constantly. She wasn't thin, but she certainly wasn't fat. She was a pretty woman with blond hair, green eyes, dimples, and the mistaken idea that her life would be much better if only she lost twenty pounds. Somehow it didn't matter what she weighed. She was always twenty pounds away from happiness.

"I'll hide them from you," Faith said.

"Thanks."

Aside from her obsession with her weight, Janine

was the perfect roommate. Since she worked in the administrative offices of the National Institutes of Health, Janine was always around to take care of things like paying bills and feeding the cat, no matter where Faith happened to be. Everything—the apartment, utilities, telephone—was in Janine's name, since Faith was out of the country so often. She was usually gone for weeks and months at a time.

More than a dependable roommate, Janine was a nice, fun person who didn't try to set Faith up on blind dates—at least, not anymore—or needle her about why she was still single at the age of thirty-three.

Faith could certainly afford a place of her own, but she liked knowing someone was there at the apartment, taking care of the details of everyday life. And she liked having a friend to come home to.

A shopper ahead had parked her cart sideways in the aisle, in front of the baby food. A toddler sat in the basket seat as the woman studied the labels on two bottles of juice.

"Excuse us," Janine said brightly as she gently shifted the tail end of the woman's cart.

"Sorry," the harried mother said, moving the cart a few inches farther toward the shelves.

Faith looked not at Janine or the other shopper, but at the little boy sitting in the cart's seat. He smiled up at her and then swiped at his runny nose.

Her thirty-third birthday had passed while she'd been working in India. It had gone by with no celebration, no cards, no gifts. She and her team had been knee-deep in patients at the time.

She had noted the date, and in a strange way it had been a sad day. Thirty-three. She was now leaving her early thirties and entering her *mid*-thirties. Biologically

she was no different than she had been two months
ago, but still it seemed like a dark milestone. She
didn't miss having a husband; she didn't pine for love
and romance. Love and romance were not for women
like her. She was too ordinary to enchant adoring men,
too dedicated to her work to waste time primping and
shopping for attractive clothes. And she wouldn't pretend to be someone she was not, dumbing down and
dressing up for the sake of impressing a member of
the male species.

In spite of all that, Faith was very aware that her
time to bear a child was here and would soon be gone.
The days went by so fast. They turned into weeks and
months and then years. No, Faith didn't miss having
a man in her life, but knowing that she would never
have a child caused a pang of regret she refused to
share with anyone. Even Janine.

She reached out to caress the little boy's cheek.

"Careful!" the woman holding two large, unwieldy
containers said sharply.

Faith's hand jerked back quickly.

The woman smiled. "Sorry. I didn't mean to sound
so shrill. Dylan has a cold. I wouldn't want you to get
it."

Faith touched the child's head. Her fingers fluttered
against pale blond bangs. "I don't get sick," she said
almost absently. She'd been exposed to much worse
than a runny nose, but she never became ill. When her
colleagues asked why her immune system worked so
well, she told them it was because she ate a balanced
diet and exercised moderately. In truth, she suspected
the strength of her immune system was a genetic trait.
Since she did not remember anything about her real

parents, she never mentioned this supposition. It could never be anything more than a theory.

Faith continued to stroke the child's hair. When she was assured that Dylan didn't object to her touch, she gently tipped his head back to take a quick peek up his nose. "He doesn't have a cold. He has allergies."

"What?"

"Your son doesn't have a cold. It's allergies."

The woman blinked twice. "Are you sure?"

"Trust her," Janine said, pushing on to the end of the aisle. "She's never wrong."

"Are you a doctor or a psychic?" the mother asked with a wry smile.

Faith returned the smile. "Doctor." She stepped toward the woman and tapped a fingertip against one of the juice containers the woman held. "And this is your best choice. In spite of the labeling, that other brand is only twenty-percent juice. It's mostly sugar water."

"Thanks." The woman squinted at the labels, then placed the rejected brand on the shelf. "Allergies, huh?"

"Don't worry. It's nothing serious. His doctor can prescribe something that will help."

"Faith," Janine called, her voice lightly touched with impatience. "The ice cream awaits."

"Good luck," Faith said as she joined her roommate. The little boy watched her go, sticking his finger up his runny nose as he tilted his head to the side to see past his mother. She kept her eyes on Dylan until she rounded the corner. Why did she want one of these messy, unpredictable creatures so badly? A baby would surely turn her life upside down.

Before they tackled the ice cream, Faith and Janine took a leisurely stroll down the magazine aisle. Janine flipped through periodicals filled with articles about weight loss, fashion and makeup. Faith browsed through the travel and financial magazines. She didn't care much about clothes or makeup, much to Janine's chagrin. Faith didn't wear makeup, and she wore her long, dark hair in a ponytail so it was easy to take care of and out of her face. Her clothes were chosen with practicality and comfort in mind. She was partial to blue, and on occasion made note of the fact that she possessed more clothing in that color than any other.

The outfit she wore today was one of her favorites. The matching cotton top and trousers were a lovely shade of sky-blue. Janine said the blouse was two sizes too large, but Faith did not agree.

At the end of the magazine display, she ran into a collection of tabloids. One headline, caught between a dog boy and an Elvis sighting, screamed at her. "Genetically Engineered Supermen in Hiding Since the Sixties! Where Are They Now?" She laughed and moved on.

"What's so funny?" Janine asked as she joined Faith, two fashion magazines added to their purchases.

Faith pointed. "'Genetically Engineered Supermen.' Where do these rags get that stuff?"

Janine shook her head. "Oh, that's been all over the news, not just in the tabloids."

Faith glanced at her roommate. "You're kidding."

"The Genetics Division is all atwitter," Janine added with a wave of her hand and a roll of her eyes. "But from what I've seen in the newspaper, they don't have anything concrete. Just some old stories and a few impossible-to-decipher files and conjecture. Mostly conjecture, from what I read."

Genetic engineering had made great strides in the past few years, but in the sixties? Impossible.

Still, the news sent a shiver dancing down Faith's spine. She wasn't sure why. True, she had no memory of her life before her real parents had been killed in a car accident. She'd been ten years old at the time. The Martins had taken her in, as they'd taken Nash in a couple of years before her. They had been the only parents she wanted or needed, until their deaths. Alice Martin had passed away four years ago from a heart attack; Elliot Martin had followed his beloved wife less than a year later. In spite of her medical training and tendency to explain everything to excess, Faith believed that her father had died of a broken heart.

Nash, her adoptive brother, was the only family she had left. A successful sculptor by trade, he was thirty-five years old but had not yet grown up. At least, not entirely. She loved him, anyway.

It was easy to imagine all sorts of fantastic things, when you couldn't remember where you came from. As a child, she had spent many nights fantasizing about who her birth parents had been, where she had come from. She'd imagined that she might be a long-lost princess. Many nights she'd wondered if perhaps her parents had survived the car crash and were desperately trying to find her.

Maybe something horrible had happened to her to make her forget her life before the age of ten.

Thirty-three was a little old for fantasy of any kind. Besides, genetically engineered supermen? Ridiculous.

Absurd tabloid tales dismissed, a pint of rocky road ice cream was added to the cart.

Janine opened the freezer door and plucked out a

carton. "Fat-free and sugar-free," she said. "Think it's any good?"

Their eyes met, and after a short pause they both shook their heads. Janine added a disgusted "Nah," and replaced the container on a freezer shelf.

They were carefully perusing the other selections when Faith's cell phone rang.

"Don't answer that!" Janine ordered.

Faith grimaced. As much as she was enjoying this outing, she didn't have much choice. She snagged the cell phone from her purse and flicked the button to answer. "Faith Martin."

"I'm glad I caught you," the tinny voice said. Teddy Lipman's high-pitched tone was unmistakable, even with a less than clear connection. The director's assistant delivered all the bad news. "Something's come up."

"I've been back in the country two days," Faith argued. "I haven't even spoken to my brother yet." Nash hadn't answered his phone. No telling where he was.

"I thought you might like this one," Teddy said in a lilting, teasing voice. "Of course, I can always ask Dr. Taylor and his team to step in, if you need more time to recover from your trip to India."

She sighed, unable to keep herself from asking, "Details?"

"We have an antimicrobial-resistant virus that has an entire town shut down. The virus has not yet been identified."

"Is the town quarantined?"

"Not yet."

Antimicrobial-resistant viruses were her specialty. She'd traveled all over the world studying them, developing new treatments and vaccines for drug-resistant diseases. "Where?"

"Montana."

That bit of news made her forget everything else. Suddenly she didn't need time off to recover from her last trip. "Here? In the States?"

"The state medical examiner ordered an autopsy on the first two victims. He was stumped, so he called us. Dr. White is studying the samples he sent at this moment, and so far he's every bit as stumped as the Montana Medical Examiner."

"Fascinating," Faith said softly.

Janine sighed and began to sort through the cart, taking out the cookies and ice cream and potato chips and leaving only low-fat, low-salt, low-taste food. She returned the rocky road to the freezer and laid the other things on a display of chocolate syrup in the aisle. Faith reached out and grabbed one package of cookies, as Teddy relayed a few details over the phone. She'd need something to eat on the plane, after all.

Dr. Luke Winston stood at the foot of the hospital bed and frowned at his sleeping patient.

He liked his answers straightforward and fast, and so far he had nothing concrete on this virus that had laid low a large number of Carson County residents and killed five others. Nothing. The state medical examiner was apparently having no better luck.

At first, he had thought the flu had arrived early, but he'd very quickly been proved wrong. This was no flu. Whatever the virus was, it turned nasty fast and could be deadly. Like the flu, this disease was most serious in the old and the young. Three of the five

fatal cases had been patients over sixty-five. One had
been a woman in her thirties, local artist Mary Mil-
stein. Mary had always been sickly, susceptible to the
ordinary illnesses that worked their way through a
community now and then, and she hadn't been strong
enough to fight off the virus. None of the treatments
he'd tried on her or the others had been effective. The
fifth casualty, last night's victim, had been a healthy
middle-aged man, a carpenter Luke knew very well,
and that loss had been hard to take. Very hard.

It now looked like Benjy Carter would be the next
casualty. Luke had delivered Benjy Carter into this
world six months ago. The child had not been healthy.
His mother, Angela, had lost her husband shortly after
discovering that she was pregnant. Her mental and
physical state had not been the best during her preg-
nancy. Benjy had been small at birth, and he'd had
one health problem after another since then. With time
and the proper care he might have outgrown his dif-
ficulties. He wouldn't have that chance now, and that
made Luke angry. Only a miracle would keep little
Benjy alive through the night.

White-hot rage flooded through him. How else
could he possibly handle this? He understood anger,
he embraced it. The last thing his patients and nurses
needed was to see him break down and cry.

When Angela woke, he would have to tell her that
her baby wasn't going to make it. She suffered from
the same virus, but she was healthy. She might very
well survive. The problem was, none of his patients
were getting any better. Some of them had been here
a week. How much abuse could a body take?

The Carson County Clinic was not set up to handle
an epidemic like this, but he'd done the best he could.

The north wing of the second floor was now isolated, and he and the nurses who worked here wore protective gear at all times. Normally Luke managed this clinic by himself, with one full-time nurse and a couple of part-timers. The population of Carson County was small, and he was able to fulfill his duties as County Health Commissioner and full-time doctor with no problem. Young specialists who were building their practices in Great Falls and Bozeman came to the Carson County Clinic once a week, or once a month, to see patients here. Other than that, this was Luke's town. His county. His people.

He heard Molly's strident voice far down the hallway. Heavyset, demanding, no-nonsense to the core, she was his number one nurse and had been for five years. What would he have done without her the past week? She had not only converted Betsy, the nurse who sometimes helped her out in the clinic, to a round-the-clock, indispensable assistant, she had also managed to convince two R.N.s from Bozeman to come to Carson County for the duration.

On the second floor it was just him, four nurses and seventeen critical patients.

"You can't be here, miss," Molly said.

Luke didn't move from his spot at the foot of Angela's bed. Molly could stop a tank, if she had a mind to. Whoever was attempting to enter her domain didn't have a chance.

"I said this area is restricted!" Molly said in a sharper tone.

A softer voice answered, and Luke turned his head as the door opened.

He wasn't sure what he had expected when he'd heard Molly charging down the hallway chasing an intruder, but this woman certainly wasn't it. She had wavy dark hair pulled away from her face, leaving her features stark and sharp on a pale face. Large, dark blue eyes, regal nose, full lips. She wasn't conventional, she wasn't gorgeous, but she was pretty, in a startling and unexpected way.

And she had no right to be here.

"Get out," he said sharply.

She didn't flinch. "You must be Dr. Winston. Would you prefer to talk in the hallway?" Without waiting for an answer, she turned and left the room.

Luke followed her, bursting into the hallway and yanking off his mask.

She offered her hand as if she expected him to shake it. He glared at her, keeping his gloved hands to himself. She let her hand drop.

"I'm Dr. Faith Martin," she said calmly. "I'm with the NIAID. The National Institute of Allergy and Infectious Diseases."

"I know what the NIAID is," he said tersely. "Who sent you?"

"I'm here on behalf of the National Institutes of Health. We were contacted by the Montana Medical Examiner. It appears you have an epidemic on your hands, Dr. Winston."

"I'm aware of that."

"I'm here to help."

His first instinct was to tell her to get out, that he didn't need any help.

But in truth he needed all the help he could get. Dammit.

"Where can my team set up?"

"Team?"

"There are four of us."

Molly spoke up. She was no longer annoyed with their intruder. She appeared and sounded grateful. "There are a couple of empty rooms on the south wing of this floor. I can open the divider between the rooms and move out the beds. With a little help, I can have it ready for you and your team in no time."

Dr. Martin glanced at Molly. "Thank you. That would be very helpful."

Molly smiled tiredly at Dr. Martin before she turned away. Was his best nurse turning on him? Molly didn't smile at complete strangers who came barging into their clinic. Maybe she knew they were desperate for any kind of help they could get. He certainly wasn't getting the job done.

Dr. Martin pulled a pair of latex gloves from the pocket of her coat and snapped them on with the precision of someone who does just that a hundred times a day. Without a word she walked past Luke to enter the room he'd just left. Two very ill patients rested there. Luke cursed, put his mask in place, grabbed another from the cart in the hallway and followed her.

"Dr. Martin!" he snapped as she foolishly leaned over a sleeping patient. When she glanced toward him, he waved the mask at her.

She did not take the mask. "I studied the samples and the notes that were sent to the NIAID by your state medical examiner. While I have not yet been able to identify the virus, I can tell you that it is not spread person-to-person. It's similar to a hantavirus, but is unlike any previously identified strain. It's likely all your patients came into physical contact with the host."

Dr. Martin examined the patient quickly and efficiently, all of her attention on the woman on the bed.

Her movements were graceful, her hands delicate and decidedly talented.

Once she began to examine the patient, he might as well not have been in the room, for all the mind Dr. Martin paid him. Her focus was entirely on the woman on the bed. The patient—fifty-year-old Melinda Harris—woke, and was visibly alarmed to find a strange woman hovering over her.

"Melinda," Luke said through his mask. Taking in what Dr. Martin had told him, he removed the mask. "This is Dr. Martin. She's here to take care of you."

The invading doctor cast him a quick glance. Of course Dr. Faith Martin wasn't actually going to take care of anyone. She was here to poke and prod and treat his patients as if they were lab rats. But he wasn't about to alarm his patient by telling her the truth.

To his surprise, Dr. Martin took Melinda's hand. "How are you feeling?" she asked.

"Terrible," Melinda croaked.

"Is your throat sore?"

The older woman nodded her head.

No one had to ask about the trouble Melinda had breathing. She rattled and coughed.

Dr. Martin continued. "Muscle ache? Sharp headache here?" She pointed to the back of her own head. After each question Melinda nodded. "That's very helpful." The doctor straightened the covers over the woman on the bed. "In just a little while, my associate is going to draw some blood. Is that all right?"

Again Melinda nodded obediently.

"We're going to find something that will make you better as quickly as possible."

"Thank you," Melinda said hoarsely.

Luke glanced at the other bed. Angela still slept.

Thank God. He wasn't ready to tell her that her son had taken a turn for the worse: he never would be.

When Dr. Martin left the room, he followed. She removed her gloves, and he ripped his away. He tossed his gloves into a nearby trash can Molly had set up for that purpose. "What kind of a doctor are you?" he asked sharply.

She turned to face him, turning up those dark blue eyes that looked so deceptively innocent. "I'm an epidemiologist," she answered seriously as she followed his example and disposed of her gloves.

Two nurses, the new girls from Bozeman, stood at the end of the hall whispering, their heads together. They were both in their early twenties, one blond and thin, the other dark and stocky. He could never get their names straight. One was Jane and the other was Michelle. They were both angels, in Luke's mind, to come here when they didn't know what they were fighting.

Most of the patients had been given something to make them comfortable, which meant they were asleep. Jane and Michelle would check on each patient frequently, but at the moment there was nothing else they could do. The entire north wing was too much like a morgue to suit Luke.

Dr. Martin glanced up at him. "That's not what you meant, is it? When you asked what kind of doctor I was, it was an insult of some kind."

Her lack of ire pushed his buttons, big time. "I'm just a little surprised that a doctor would stand over a patient and lie the way you did. How dare you walk in here and promise my patients a cure when there isn't one! We don't even know what this is!"

"I do," she said calmly.

Her answer took him by surprise. All he could think about was how he was going to tell Angela about Benjy, that he hadn't slept more than three hours at a stretch for a full week…and that Dr. Faith Martin smelled too good.

"What is it?" He wanted to know what disease had descended upon his town and turned his neat little world upside down.

"Can we discuss this over dinner? I'm starving. Missed lunch."

"I don't have time to eat," he snapped.

She showed no visible reaction to his angry response. Her words were calm. "When was the last time you ate a meal, Dr. Winston?"

In truth, he couldn't remember when he'd last eaten sitting down. Molly handed him granola bars now and then, and kept him hydrated with bottled water. He ate and drank on the run.

"Dinner," he snapped. "Why not? I guess your *team* will keep an eye on the patients for me."

"Dr. Winston, do you have a problem with my presence here?"

He lied with a straight face. "Of course not." She'd been here a matter of minutes, and he already had problems with this woman's presence. Like it or not, he needed her help.

"Glad to hear it," she said. "As we arrived, I saw a café on the corner. Is the food there any good?"

"Fair enough."

She turned and walked away from him. "It's going to be a long night, and I'm really a bear to work with when I'm hungry."

So far Dr. Martin had been too nice. Luke had been a bear lately, but he kept telling himself that when this virus was under control everything would be better. The sad truth was, he'd been a bear for ten months, since Karen had died. Best not to let his mind go there, not today. He told the nurses on duty to call if they needed him; he had his cell phone with him at all times, as always. Jane—or was it Michelle?—nodded as Luke delivered his instructions.

The epidemiologist who had barged in and was trying to take over his clinic didn't dress provocatively. Her sweater and trousers were loose, dark green and warm enough for a Montana October. Her hair, interesting as it was, hadn't been teased, curled and sprayed into submission. As far as he could tell, she wore no makeup. Then again, she didn't exactly need any.

Dressed down or not, she was unlike any doctor he had ever met.

She had one apparent feminine wile. That scent of hers left a trail wherever she went, like a sweet trap or a very gentle come-hither. Well, he wasn't falling for it. In another time and another place, maybe. But he had his hands full at the moment, and as lovely as the scent was, it bugged the hell out of him.

"Dr. Martin," he said in a businesslike tone of voice as he followed her to the elevator. "Several of my patients are allergic to perfume."

"I assure you that has nothing to do with the virus," she said pragmatically.

He gritted his teeth. "I know that. It's just that while you're working here, perhaps you shouldn't wear any."

She glanced in his direction as they stepped onto the elevator, a puzzled expression flitting across her oddly pretty face. "I never do."

Crap.

# Two

The café that Dr. Winston said served "fair enough" food was one of those wonderful mom-and-pop places. Small, out-of-the-way restaurants that served fabulous food was something else Faith missed when she traveled outside of the country. The sweet and spicy aromas filling the air were fabulous. She was certain dinner would be heavenly.

She traveled frequently, but she'd never been to Montana. So far, she was impressed with the landscape and *most* of the people. Rockland was a small, quaint town, with mountains to one side and vast plains to the other, magnificent and wild, soothing in a gut-deep way. And the people had all been warm and welcoming.

Well, with one very obvious exception.

The local doctor had been kept busy since they'd ordered their meals, answering questions from concerned townsfolk. It was rather interesting to watch. The people who gathered around the table called him Luke, not Dr. Winston, but the respect they had for him was evident. He was straightforward with them, answering their questions truthfully while being very careful not to scare anyone. He introduced her as Dr. Martin, and said she had come to help. Nothing more. They nodded politely and thanked her.

Dr. Winston was one of those physicians who cared

for their patients in a very personal way. He felt each pain, and beat himself up over every failure. She had known him less than an hour, and yet she was certain he grieved for every patient he'd ever lost.

That was a luxury she could not afford.

As huge plates laden with meat loaf, green beans, corn pudding and rolls were placed before them, the people who had gathered around to ask questions about the epidemic backed away one at a time. Several of them thanked her again for coming to their aid.

"All right," Dr. Winston said as he forked up a piece of meat loaf. He kept his voice purposely low so as not to alarm any of the other patrons. "What is it? Tell me exactly what this damned disease is."

"It's similar to a hantavirus, but we haven't been able to identify the exact strain. There are, in fact, some indications that it might be something entirely new. By the time we return, the lab will be set up and I can conduct further tests. We need a detailed genetic analysis before we can continue."

"But you said you knew what it was."

"I believe I do, though it does seem to have mutated. There's a yellowish tinge to the fingernails, and an unusual discoloration about the eyes that leads me to believe it's a particular virus. And as I said, it isn't spread from person to person."

"Are you sure about that?" he asked.

Faith was not accustomed to being questioned. "Have any of your staff become ill?" she asked.

Dr. Winston shook his head. "No. We've been careful. And lucky."

"It's not luck," she said. "In order to contract the virus, you have to come into direct contact with the contagion by either breathing the particles or touching them directly so that they're absorbed through the skin.''

"It's spreading quickly enough," he grumbled. "I have seventeen patients in my clinic. Seventeen! Add the five casualties and we're talking about twenty-two people who have been infected. Twenty-two, in a very sparsely populated county. They all became ill over a period of four days. Some of them live miles apart. How do you explain that?''

"I can't, not yet," Faith let the puzzle settle in her mind. Each epidemic was a puzzle, a deadly riddle, and it was her job to make the pieces fit. "We're going to have to get local law enforcement involved. Have the homes and workplaces of your patients been examined?''

"Our local law enforcement is a sheriff who should've retired two elections ago and a handful of inept, underpaid, very young deputies," Dr. Winston said impatiently. "They have their hands full dealing with the reporters who have shown up to follow the story. We can't count on them, not for anything.''

"Surely they can bring in reinforcements." Faith was horrified by the news that she would not have the assistance of the sheriff and his men. "I can instruct them on what to look for, and show them how to protect themselves as they search for the host. Commonality must be established as soon as possible." Inept or not, she would make use of whatever manpower she could find.

"Dr. Martin," the local doctor began, shaking his head as if he had arguments for her perfectly sensible plan.

She was in no mood to argue. "I can call in military support.''

The widening of his eyes revealed his reaction to this suggestion. ''Military support?''

''If necessary.''

He shook off the concerns. ''Right now I just want to get my patients stable. I can't treat the disease if I don't know what it is. Until now we've just been treating the symptoms. You can do more, right?''

''After I conduct a few preliminary tests, yes.''

He seemed relieved by this news, so much so that his entire face changed. Softened just slightly. He was tired and angry and confused by the changes that had swept through the town with the virus. For a moment, Faith felt genuinely sorry for the doctor.

Dr. Luke Winston was a good-looking man, she observed indifferently. He could use a haircut. Brown hair curled around his collar and over his ears. She suspected his shaggy hairstyle and stubbly jaw were due to a lack of time for a visit to the barbershop, rather than a fashion statement. He had very nice blue eyes and symmetrical masculine features. He would definitely be handsome if he'd get that sour expression off his face! Of course, handling an epidemic of any kind was difficult for a physician, especially one like Luke Winston. He was under a lot of strain, and it showed.

''When will you be able to tell me what it is? I want you to give this virus a name for me. Something besides Rockland Fever, which is what the damn newspapers have been calling it.'' He sounded as if he thought if he had a name, he could curse the disease back to where it had come from.

''What I've seen thus far is similar to a microbe that was named *Muerto Canyon*, in 1994, but of course until I do more tests I can't label the virus at all.''

"*Muerto Canyon?* What does that mean?"

"The Valley of Death," she translated.

He paled visibly.

"The majority of those infected will be able to fight off the virus," she assured him. "Once we have a treatment formulated and the culprit eliminated, we should be able to bring this to a quick and sure halt."

He nodded.

"We've done this before," she said gently. "Everything's going to be fine."

He lifted his head to glare at her, his jaw tightening and his lips growing thin and hard. At that moment, his eyes were almost electric blue. There was definitely fire there. "Dr. Martin, I don't need you to reassure me like I'm some kind of rube who doesn't know his ass from a hole in the ground. Save the kindhearted consolations for someone who needs them."

"You would prefer our discussions to remain strictly professional," she said, not allowing her feelings to be hurt by his rejection. She didn't have time for such nonsense. So Dr. Luke Winston was a jerk. He wasn't the first jerk she'd met; he wouldn't be the last.

"Yes."

"Fine. When we return to the clinic, perhaps you could compile a list of your patients, the day they became ill, and their home and work addresses. If any of your patients have ties with one another, if they're neighbors, if they work together, then I need a note of that, too. Connectivity, Doctor, that is our first responsibility. We must establish connectivity."

"It hit six people at once, and I had five new patients the next day," Dr. Winston interrupted. "Seven the third day, four the fourth. There have been no new cases since then, but until we know what it is and where it came from, I can't rest easy.''

"The source of the disease must be identified as quickly as possible.'' She didn't want to imagine what would happen if this virus spread. If they could not identify the source, that could very easily happen. "It's too late in the season for a mosquito-transmitted disease in this part of the country, so we must look at mice, birds and sheep first. We must find the host and eliminate or contain it.''

"What if we can't?'' Dr. Winston asked sharply. "What if we don't find the origin of this disease?''

Faith didn't believe in pulling punches. "We could very easily have a national emergency on our hands.''

He wouldn't admit it to Dr. Martin, but he did feel better. The meal had done him good, and so had getting out of the clinic for a breath of fresh air. As they walked back to the clinic they moved quickly. October in Montana was cold, especially once the sun set.

A few strands of the good doctor's ponytail had come undone so that several waving locks fell over her shoulder and down her back, but she seemed unaware of the fact. Faith Martin seemed unaware of many things, to be honest, as if she lived in her own little world. There were no outward signs that she took time to pretty herself up, and yet she smelled good. No perfume, or so she said. She used scented shampoo, maybe, or a special scented soap that tested the patience of any man who came near, without openly tempting him.

Dr. Martin moved gracefully, but completely without artifice. She didn't have what anyone would call a mouthwatering figure. In fact, she was almost flat chested. Almost. Her curves were small but nice, and she definitely didn't dress to show off what shape she possessed. She was delicate and yet strong, attractive and yet completely ignorant of her striking looks.

Luke shook off his unexpected fascination with the woman; anything he felt right now was simply the effect of not enough sleep and too much emotional turmoil. He roped in his stray thoughts as they neared the clinic.

For a small town, Rockland was lucky to have such a well-equipped clinic. Much of the equipment and supplies had been purchased through donations from the two guest ranches outside the city limits. The owners said it made their guests feel safer when they spent a week or two in the summer pretending to be cowboys. Since one of those ranch owners had five sons, all of them involved in the rodeo in some way, a nearby medical facility was definitely a good thing.

The clinic looked plain from the outside, squat, square and constructed of yellow brick. Inside, the first floor was comprised of a large lobby, rest rooms, a snack area with a few tables and vending machines, and the offices where Luke normally saw his patients.

The second floor was similar to a small hospital floor, complete with nurses' station, patient rooms and Luke's personal office. Until recently, the facilities had not been put to the test. In the past week, however, they'd been strained to the limit.

A trio of reporters milled about restlessly in the lobby. Luke wondered if the others who had been gathering here for the past few days had decided they'd gotten all they were going to get out of this story, and had finally gone home. If so, things would be quiet again at the Rockland Motel, which never saw this kind of business after the summer, like everyone else around here.

The three reporters who remained in the lobby all looked bored and tired. A couple of them, the red-headed woman and a man, had been here all week. The shapely blonde from Great Falls had only been hanging around for three or four days. As soon as word had leaked out that there was an epidemic in Carson County, small Rockland had become news. Not big news, but news just the same.

The reporters became alert at the appearance of the two doctors.

"Hey, Dr. Winston," the redhead called, flashing them a tired smile as she stepped forward. "Who's your friend?"

He ignored the query, as he ignored all the questions the reporters threw at him. Anything to report? Is it true that the government is now involved? Have you identified the disease, yet?

A sheriff's deputy had been on duty in the lobby for the past five days, to keep reporters and anyone else who didn't belong away from the second floor. It was amazing to Luke that it was necessary to have a guard to keep people away from a deadly disease. Until Dr. Martin's arrival, no one here had realized that the virus didn't spread from person to person, and still the reporters had gotten too close. One deputy had caught the male reporter who was still here, an annoying man from Billings, trying to sneak up the stairs at least once that Luke knew of. What some people would do for a story.

When the elevator doors closed, Luke was grateful for the immediate silence.

There was no conversation as they rode to the second floor. Dr. Martin's mind was definitely elsewhere. Luke was in no mood for idle chitchat. When they reached the second floor and the elevator doors opened, a short, balding man in a white lab coat was waiting for them.

"You really must see this," the man said in an excited voice, his attention entirely on Dr. Martin. Luke felt momentarily invisible.

The man led the way to the end of the hall, where the partition between two rooms had been opened. Beds had been taken out, tables and sophisticated laboratory equipment brought in. While they'd been eating, Molly and Dr. Martin's team had been busy setting up a functional lab. Luke was amazed that they'd been able to work so quickly.

"Hello." One of the doctors approached Luke with a hesitant smile. He was tall, thin, blond and wearing a white lab coat over dark trousers. "I'm Dr. Willis Helm. Thank you so much for inviting us in."

Luke refrained from informing Dr. Helm that he had not been invited.

"That's Dr. Larry Gant," Helm continued, pointing at the excited man who had met Luke and Dr. Martin at the elevator. "And that—" he indicated a dark-haired man about Luke's age who was presently pushing his glasses up on his nose and staring intently at the only woman in their group "—is Dr. John White. We're all very excited to be here."

Very excited. He was burying his patients, and these nerds were *very excited*.

Luke shook his head. He could tell Helm had meant no offense. The doctor was just a world-class geek in a room full of world-class geeks. He would leave the lab work to Dr. Martin and her crew. All Luke wanted was another look at Benjy. "I have a patient..." he began.

Dr. Martin silenced him with a single raised finger. She didn't even look at him as she donned a lab coat and pulled on the proper protective gear before approaching the microscope.

Luke leaned against the door, amused and chagrined at the same time. Who the hell did she think she was?

His trace of amusement died when Dr. Martin lifted her head, laying her eyes on him for the briefest split second.

"What's wrong?" he asked, pushing away and standing up straight. "Is this thing what you thought it would be?"

"Not exactly." She turned to her colleague. "It's similar to a hantavirus, but this is definitely something different. Perhaps new, as we suspected. But I believe it can be treated with a megadose of a new antibiotic."

"I've given my patients antibiotics," Luke protested.

"This is a specific antibiotic and a specific dose. I've been developing it for months, and it's designed to fight diseases that do not respond to traditional treatment. Unfortunately I don't have a great deal of the antibiotic with me. Who are your most critical patients?"

*Benjy.* "A six-month-old who was in ill health before he contracted the disease, and two elderly sisters."

"They'll be first," she said, ripping off her gloves and disposing of them in a mindless manner. "I can have more of the antibiotic flown in by morning."

"Wait just a minute," Luke said as he followed the maddening woman out the door and into the hallway.

"I appreciate the fact that you're here to help, but I won't allow you to come into my hospital and start treating my patients with experimental drugs without even consulting—"

She spun on him. If he hadn't been paying very close attention, he would have run her over. "You have no idea what you're dealing with," she said in a lowered voice. "What I've found thus far is not exactly what I expected, but I am certainly more familiar with the mechanics of an epidemic that you are."

"That doesn't mean—"

"Compile that list we talked about over dinner and then go home, Dr. Winston," she said calmly. "I'll have a nurse call if I need you."

"I will not go home," he said, leaning down to place his face closer to hers. Faith Martin was about five foot seven, maybe a little taller, and he didn't have to lean over very far. Her scent was intense when he stood this close. Some fancy shampoo, he decided, if she'd been telling the truth and really wasn't wearing perfume.

He hadn't been this close to a woman who wasn't a patient since Karen had died. That was why Dr. Martin smelled good. That was why she made something in his gut react in a perfectly understandable way. He ignored the smell, his gut, and the way his fingers itched.

"These are my patients," he said sternly, "this is my clinic, and—"

"No," she said, completely unaffected by his intimidating posture. "By the authority of the federal government, these are now my patients and this is my clinic. Go home. You look like you haven't slept in a week."

"Dr. Martin," he seethed, "I am not going home."

"Dr. Winston," she countered calmly, "when you pass out from sheer exhaustion, neither my associates nor I will be able to take care of you. We have more important things to do here."

"I don't need anyone to take care of me," he answered.

"Do what you want, then," she said, before turning her back on him. "I don't have time to argue with you anymore."

She was almost at the end of the hallway when she muttered, "Jackass."

Such a common word coming out of such a prim, serious mouth made Luke grin for the first time since this disease had shown up in his county.

The smile didn't last long.

It was well past midnight when Faith stepped into the baby's room. At last check, the child had been responding well to the antibiotic treatment. A quick peek to make sure all was still well, that was what she intended. There were two other affected children in another hospital room, but the more severely ill Benjy had a room to himself. One of the nurses was always with him. None of the R.N.s working in the Carson County Clinic had any specific training on the care of critically ill infants, but they were doing a fine job.

Tonight there was no nurse on duty in Benjy's room. Dr. Winston sat in the rocking chair by the baby bed. Benjy, swaddled in a blue blanket so that everything but his little face was covered, slept in the arms of his doctor.

Dr. Winston lifted his head slowly, and Faith prepared herself for another argument. The man was im-

possible! He seemed determined to fight her every step
of the way. Well, she could be just as bullheaded as
he, if the situation called for such a response.

Faith's plans to meet Dr. Winston head-on died
rather quickly. It was difficult to remain angry with a
man who held a small child this way—with strength
and tenderness. Maybe it wasn't always a bad thing to
care too much for one's patients. If he wanted to rail
against her for coming in and taking over, she could
take it. Maybe venting would make him feel better.

"Thank you," he said, his voice soft and deep.

His thanks took her by surprise, and she was at a
loss as to how to answer. Finally she said, "He's responding very well. We shouldn't get our hopes up.
This is a treatment. We can't know yet whether or not
it is a *cure*. The success of the treatment does buy us
some badly needed time. And with the information on
the patients you compiled so quickly, we'll be able to
track and eradicate the source of the virus."

Dr. Martin looked down at the baby. The lights in
the room were low, so his expression was shaded, a
dark shadow hiding much of his face from her. "When
you arrived this afternoon, I was trying to come up
with an acceptable way to tell Benjy's mother that he
was dying. Thanks to you, I won't have to."

"I'm just doing my job, Dr. Winston," she replied,
uneasy with his gratitude.

"Luke," he said. "Call me Luke. Everyone else
does."

Calling him by his first name would be much too
personal. The very idea gave her cold feet.

She would bring the epidemic under control, treat
the patients as needed and study the virus. Perhaps
there would be an opportunity to research and develop

a vaccine, in case this virus should spread, but that sort of research usually took years. Her job here was to stop the spread of the disease before it got out of hand. When that was done, she'd leave this cold little Montana town for another disaster site. That was her life. She did not make friends along the way, nor did she find herself admiring country doctors who took every case to heart. But Luke Winston asked so sincerely, and he cared so deeply....

"All right," she said. "Luke. Now will you go home and get some sleep? You truly do look terrible."

He lifted his head and looked at her. "How do you know I don't look this terrible all the time?"

"Just a hunch," she answered.

Dr. Winston—Luke—stood carefully and laid Benjy in his bed. His hands were large, especially when compared to the size of the child. But those hands were capable, talented and caring. The baby stirred but did not awake.

"Maybe you're right," Luke said. "I want to get scrubbed up, put on some clean clothes, go home and hug my daughter. Then maybe I'll sleep."

Her heart sank, just a little. A daughter. Of course he was married! Men like Luke Winston didn't live alone. They didn't dedicate themselves to their work, to the exclusion of all else.

"Your wife must be frantic, with all the hours you've been away from home lately," Faith said casually. "I'm sure she'll be glad to see you."

Even in the dim light, she could see the sudden and distinct change in Luke's expression. There was no longer any ease on his face or in the way he held his body. "My wife is dead," he said simply.

"I'm sorry," she whispered.

He didn't offer any details. How long had he been a widower? To lose a wife so young was surely horrible. Faith could only imagine what it would be like to love someone so much and then watch them die.

It was obvious that Luke did not want to talk about his late wife. He ambled toward the door. "I'll be back tomorrow morning, bright and early," he said, his eyes on the door.

"No rush," Faith said. "Take whatever time you need. Tomorrow morning the new shipment will arrive via military helicopter and all the patients will receive the antibiotic treatment. Once that's done, we'll concentrate on finding the source and completing the genetic analysis of the virus."

"In other words, you don't need me here," he said as he came to a stop beside her.

"That's not what I said."

Luke looked down at her, and the inflexibility she had seen in him just a moment ago was gone. He remained tired, though. In fact, he was dancing on the edge of sheer exhaustion. This man needed a shave, a haircut, a shower and a couple days of sleep. So why was there still an indefinable strength in him? If she wasn't here, if Benjy hadn't taken a good turn, if he thought his presence in this clinic would serve any purpose at all, he would be here through the night. Again.

His eyes flitted over the lines of her face, then finally found and held her eyes. He didn't turn away, didn't move his gaze to a safer, more polite place. Neither did she. Faith held her breath. No one had ever stared at her quite this way, as a man might stare at a woman he found interesting.

"Does anyone call you Faith? Or are you always

Dr. Martin?'' He didn't wait for an answer. ''You look more like a Faith than a Dr. Martin, especially in this light, with those big eyes and that cute nose and all that hair. You have great hair, by the way.''

Her first response was not at all appropriate. *My nose is not cute.* At least she managed to stop the words before they poured out of her mouth. ''Dr.— Luke,'' she said, ''this really isn't—''

''Don't tell me,'' he interrupted. ''I'm out of line. I'm behaving badly. This is very unprofessional of me. You're going to have someone come drag me away and toss me in jail for telling you that you have great hair.''

''Of course not.''

''The truth is, you were right all along. About the treatment, about the disease itself, about the fact that I need to get out of here and get some sleep. I have a feeling you're one of those women who's *always* right. Doesn't that get boring after a while?''

She opened her mouth to tell him to stop this, but she didn't have a chance to speak.

''I'm tired. No, I'm way beyond tired. I'm punchy and weaving and…empty.'' A half smile flitted across his face. ''I'm so out of it, I open my mouth and whatever's on my mind just spills out. Did I tell you that you smell good?''

''Dr. Winston,'' Faith said sharply, taking a single step back, ''this is entirely inappropriate.''

''I know,'' he said. ''Maybe tomorrow I'll care.'' He ambled toward the door. ''Maybe not.'' He opened the door and, without glancing back, said, ''Good night, Dr. Martin.''

The door swung closed and Luke was well down
the hall before she realized that she should have in-
structed him to call her Faith. Too late. The moment
had come and gone.

# Three

Since coming to Carson County five years ago, Luke had lived in a cabin within walking distance of the clinic. He'd loved that house from the first time he'd walked through the front door. His home was solid, warm, big enough to suit him, but not too big.

A memory he'd rather forget teased him. Karen had hated the log house. She'd sometimes talked about building something nicer, something befitting his position. More often she'd talked about moving to the city, being a *real* doctor's wife, spending the big bucks he would make in a big hospital. She'd hated it here. He hadn't realized how much until it was too late.

Luke tried to push aside the memory of his last conversation with his wife, the day she'd died. Thinking about what he could have done differently, what he *should* have done, was his own brand of self-inflicted torture. The guilt he suffered wasn't as bad as it had been in the first three months following Karen's passing, but it was still with him. Every day, every night.

He drew in a deep breath of cold air as he walked to the clinic in the morning light. He could almost smell the coming snow on the wind. Many of the places he'd lived while growing up didn't see snow all year, much less this early in the fall. Texas, Florida, Mississippi. But then there had been years when they'd lived in Virginia and Michigan, and he did see

snow. He'd never known where he'd be, from one year
to the next.

Maybe that was why he loved his home here so
much. His electrician father had traveled constantly,
taking his family where the work was. Rockland was
home, the first real home he'd ever known. He loved
it here. He'd put down solid roots and hadn't been
willing to give them up for Karen.

The memories he tried to push deep came surging
back. Would his wife still be alive if he'd given in to
her demands and left Carson County behind years
ago?

Straight ahead the clinic loomed before him, and
Luke turned his mind to more immediate problems.
He remembered last night's conversation with Dr.
Martin, but he wished he didn't. He was a grade-A
nitwit. She'd probably had him barred from the second
floor! The military she'd threatened to call in was
probably already in position and would keep him out.

No way. It didn't matter who Dr. Martin was, or
what kind of power she wielded. The people in that
clinic were still his patients. He needed help, but he
did not need a bossy woman to come in and take over.

Luke unnecessarily prepared himself for battle. The
deputy at the elevator tipped his hat and said good-
morning. There were no armed soldiers waiting to stop
him on the second floor. Apparently there had been
no command to shoot him on sight.

The vision of Faith Martin, standing toe to toe with
Sheriff Talbot, was intriguing enough to make him
smile. Talbot was six foot three, overweight, balding
and lazy. Dr. Martin had her feet planted and her chin
tipped up to look the lawman in the eye. A white lab
coat draped her slender body; Talbot was in khaki

strained to the max, as usual. They had been arguing. She was winning. Luke could tell by the red splotches on the sheriff's face.

A good night's sleep hadn't dulled Luke's fascination with Dr. Martin. He was still oddly drawn to her. She certainly hadn't had a good night's sleep. Under her lab coat, those were the same clothes she'd been wearing last night, baggy, shapeless and dull green. Had she spent all night in her laboratory? Or had she passed the hours looking in on and treating his patients?

He might have spoken too freely last night, but he'd been right about at least one thing. The name Faith suited this woman much more than a stern and impersonal Dr. Martin. A Faith would take down her hair and shake it out. A Faith would smile now and then. A Faith would be soft and gentle, at the right time and place. Luke closed his eyes. This wasn't right; not here, not now.

Maybe Nelda, his nanny and housekeeper, wasn't full of crap after all. She kept telling him that one day he'd wake up and realize that it wasn't natural for a healthy thirty-seven-year-old man to live alone. She also kept telling him that Abby needed a mother, that he needed a wife, that one of these days he was going to forget and forgive the past and move on.

He'd fire that meddling Nelda today, if Abby didn't love her so much.

As he stepped closer to Dr. Martin, he could hear the conversation. "You don't have any choice, Sheriff," Faith said in a surprisingly strong voice.

"Little lady, I told you a hundred times, I don't have the manpower to go poking around the homes of twenty-two sick people looking for dead critters."

Luke wondered if she'd smack the sheriff for calling her "little lady."

"Find the manpower," she insisted. "I don't care if you beg, borrow or steal it. And tell your men you are most likely looking for infected birds or mice. It's imperative that they wear protective gloves, masks and gowns at all times."

The sheriff began again. "I don't—"

"I'm sure you realize that twenty-two infected does not equal twenty-two residences. Many of those who were afflicted lived in the same home. A mother and son, sisters, a husband and wife. But you do need to also inspect the workplaces of those who became ill."

"There's no way!" Talbot thundered.

"Fine," Faith said calmly. "I'll call the governor and tell him the sheriff's department here in Carson County is inadequate. I'm sure there are ways in which he can assist you."

Talbot took a step back. He obviously did not want the governor's attentions turned in his direction. "I'll see what I can do."

"Today," Faith insisted.

The lawman grumbled, "Today."

Luke joined them. The confrontation was over. Faith had won. He was not surprised. "Good morning," he said.

The sheriff glared at him. "Doctor," he said curtly, and then he stalked toward the elevator.

Luke looked down at Faith. There were circles under her eyes, an unnatural paleness to her cheeks. "What's wrong?" he asked.

"Nothing," she insisted.

He shook his head. "You send me home and order

me to get some sleep, and then you stay here and work all night.''

A new element had been added to her tired face. Frustration. "There's something odd about this virus," she said softly. "No matter which way I look at it, it's just not as it should be."

"I think it's time for you to get some sleep." Luke took her arm and tried to lead her toward the elevator. "Do you have a room at the motel?" Carson County's poor excuse for visitor lodging was twelve shabby rooms. Each room had one double bed and mismatched furniture and opened onto a small parking lot. The Rockland Motel wasn't fancy, but Faith didn't need fancy right now. She needed a bed and a few hours of peace and quiet.

"Yes, but—"

"No buts. Get some rest and everything will look different when you get back." He smiled at her. "I promise you."

She still balked. "The shipment of antibiotics will be delivered in three hours, and I need to be here. I also need to take another look at the last specimen—"

Stubborn woman! "Dammit, Fai—Dr. Martin," he corrected himself quickly. Not quickly enough. "Take your own advice. No one around here will be available to take care of you if you pass out from exhaustion."

"I do this for a living," she insisted. "I've gone days without sleep with no ill effects. I certainly don't need you telling me how to take care of myself in this situation."

He dropped his hand from her arm. "Fine. Work yourself into the ground. Just don't make a mistake on one of my patients because you're sleep deprived."

She looked rightfully insulted. "I do not make mistakes."

"I'm sure you don't."

"I am exceedingly cautious."

"Of course you are."

She didn't stalk away from him, as she should have. Argument over, she had won again, Luke thought.

"If you change your mind," he said, "there's a cot in my office. It's much more private and quiet than the patient rooms, but you'd be right here, close to the action."

Something on her face softened just slightly. "I am very tired. Maybe I can make use of that cot for a couple of hours. Would you wake me when the antibiotic arrives?"

"Of course, Dr. Martin."

She brushed back a strand of dark hair with a delicate hand. Her mouth twitched a little, and she cut her eyes to the side almost shyly. "You can call me Faith," she said absently.

Why did he believe that this was a huge gesture, coming from her? The men she worked with, the trio of nerds, all called her Dr. Martin. She didn't seem to mind.

"I will," he said.


A two-hour nap later, Faith felt refreshed and renewed. She should have grabbed a few hours of sleep last night, but the virus had kept her awake. Something was wrong. This disease acted like a hantavirus, but it wasn't. A mutating virus could be a very bad thing. She suspected the contagion was transmitted by diseased birds or mice, but until she had hard evidence she would not rest easy.

Unchecked, the virus could sweep across the country. With a little luck and a lot of hard work, maybe they could contain it. Stop it. Kill it, before it killed anyone else.

Luke's outer office was tiny, but there was a small anteroom with a comfortable cot, a refrigerator and microwave, and an even smaller attached bath, complete with shower. It looked as if he lived here. Perhaps he did on occasion, when it became necessary.

According to her watch, she had about a half an hour before the antibiotic arrived. The thought of a shower was more than good; the longer she imagined the feel of hot water spraying onto her skin, the more it seemed necessary. She peeked into the bathroom and saw that there were plenty of towels, soap and shampoo. In so many of the places she'd worked in the past few years, a hot shower, complete with soap, would have been considered a luxury.

Before she could talk herself out of it, she began to take off her clothes. Ten minutes, tops, and she'd be done.

Standing under the spray felt so good, she went well beyond her ten minutes. Her mind worked even as she stood there with water running over her face. Eyes closed, body still, she processed through her mind all the information she had collected. Usually these puzzles fell together for her in an easy fashion. Not today.

Faith had seen deadlier diseases in her career, many of them. She had treated more severely afflicted patients than those at the Carson County Clinic. But she had never studied a virus that perplexed her as this one did.

She left the shower, grabbing a large white towel to dry herself with. As she briskly dried her skin, she looked at her discarded clothes and sighed. She hated to put those dirty clothes on her clean body, but there wasn't anything to be done for it.

Unless Luke kept clean scrubs in his office. That he would do so made sense, considering the other amenities here. Her hair towel-dried and hanging over her shoulders, Faith wrapped herself in the soft white towel and stepped out of the bathroom. Where would Luke store extra scrubs? She glanced around the room quickly. On one side of the room there sat a small countertop with cabinets above and below. It was the only logical place to look.

She had gone through all the top cabinets and was bending over, reaching for the lower cabinet on the right side, when the door swung open without warning. "Wake up. Your—" Luke stopped speaking abruptly, just as Faith stood and spun around to face him.

He stared at her. "Your shipment has arrived."

"Thank you," Faith said, holding the towel tightly to make sure it remained closed. It didn't cover enough, but she was decent. From breast to thigh, the white terry cloth covered her. She stood tall and maintained a somewhat professional demeanor. In many third world countries, where she worked and lived for months on end, modesty was not only silly, it was impossible. So why did she feel the heat of a blush rise to her cheeks now? "I was looking for scrubs. Do you have any here?" She saw no reason to explain to Luke that the clothes she'd worn all day yesterday and last night did not appeal to her at the moment.

"Sure. Far left cabinet on the bottom. Help yourself."

"Thank you."

Luke stood there watching her for a moment longer, then turned to leave the room. Finally!

It wasn't until after he was gone that Faith realized her heart was beating too hard and her respiration was irregular. Her face was warm, as if she continued to blush, and there was a strange tingling in her toes and in the depths of her chest.

If she didn't know better, she'd think she was coming down with something.

Luke wondered if anyone had ever told Dr. Faith Martin that she had a nice ass. Probably not. She probably dated guys who had more class than he did. Guys who gave her polite compliments and took her to dinner and maybe on the third date stole a passionless kiss.

No, that was wrong. Faith didn't date *guys,* he was sure of it. She dated professional men who were as uptight as she was.

He wanted to tell her she had a nice ass. After all, he'd walked into the room and seen a good portion of it as she'd bent over to open a cabinet.

On the outside, Faith Martin put on a good show of being efficiently detached and unemotional, all work and no play, a woman who never thought of anything but her work. Though she'd been here less than twenty-four hours, he knew better.

Luke shook off the unexpected and inexplicable attraction to the doctor who was presently administering her newly developed antibiotic to his patients. It had been ten months since Karen had died, more than a year since he'd last had sex. That was all this was. Sexual desire. Physical need. The wrong woman at the wrong time.

He had a feeling Faith Martin didn't go in for casual sex while she was on the job. She probably didn't go in for casual sex at any time. She was too old to be a virgin…wasn't she? But she was definitely virginal. Aloof. What man could break through that ice to find the woman beneath? Him? Not likely. He was a dismal failure where women were concerned. His wife had come to hate him in the last years of their marriage. Had they really thought a baby would make things better? How foolish. Since Karen's death, a number of women had flirted with him, made it clear that they were available if he was interested. Not one of them had appealed to him, even though they had been, for the most part, sweet, pretty, available women.

Why Faith Martin, and why now?

She hadn't looked him in the eye since he'd walked in and caught her wearing nothing but a towel. Her still-damp hair was pulled back as she worked. The scrubs, *his* scrubs, were too big for her, but she'd managed to make them fit with an adjustment here and there.

Together they saw that all the patients were given the antibiotic treatment. Those who had received the medication last night were already much improved. There had been no new patients for four days, now. Maybe, just maybe, this was about to be over. Under control, at least. Then he could get Faith Martin out of his clinic, out of his town and out of his head.

Faith was pleased by the response to the new antibiotic. It seemed an effective treatment. While those who had been afflicted with the virus were not returning to their full state of health immediately, they were no longer critical. Now she could turn her attentions to studying the virus itself.

The sheriff claimed his men had not found evidence of dead, diseased "critters" in the homes or workplaces of any of the victims. If he didn't come up with something soon, she would be forced to call in outside authorities to conduct the search. She'd wanted to give the local government a chance first. Otherwise they always got their egos wounded. Egos aside, she could not stand by and allow the source of the virus to remain undiscovered.

But by late afternoon, she was fading. Her short nap would not carry her through the night, and she liked working at night, when she could. The hospital would be quiet, her colleagues would be sleeping, and it would be just Faith and the lab. Faith and the virus. Faith and her world.

She slipped out without telling anyone but Molly where she was going. She'd grab a bite to eat, sleep in her motel bed and then shower again and put on her own clean clothes. This time there wouldn't be anyone around to walk in on her.

In the lobby, a young deputy sat at the reception desk. He was sound asleep. She wanted to be angry at the lax security, but she knew the deputies had been working long hours, even if the sheriff had not. But without protection, the sole remaining reporter caught up with her. The redheaded woman had a huge smile on her face as she approached Faith.

Faith knew she could turn her back on the young woman and refuse to answer any questions, but the interview was inevitable. Best to get it over with.

"Hi there," the reporter said brightly. "Would you answer a few questions for me? Please?"

Faith looked around the quiet lobby. "Sure. What happened to the others?" It was a relief not to be hounded, but she had a suspicion that soon, very soon, every newspaper in the country would be interested in this story. It was intriguing. Unidentified diseases that killed always were.

"They stepped out for a bite to eat," the reporter explained.

"And you weren't hungry?"

"I asked them to bring me something back." She smiled widely. "And I'm glad I did. Otherwise, I would've missed you."

Faith took a deep breath. "I have very little time and there's not much I can tell you, but if you have a few simple questions I'd be happy to answer them. If I can," she added.

"What's your name and why are you here?" the reporter asked, her pencil poised above her notepad.

"Dr. Faith Martin, NIAID. My associates and I have come to assist Dr. Winston."

The reporter's eyes lit up. "Great! Do you have any explanations for my readers, yet? What is Rockland Fever, anyway?"

So far, the questions were easy. Simple. "I can assure you and the public that the epidemic is under control. All the patients are stable at this time. As soon as I have a more definitive answer for you, regarding the disease itself, I'll make a formal statement."

It struck Faith as odd that the reporter wrote none of this down. The woman certainly seemed interested, but she really should take notes. Faith hated to be misquoted.

The redhead leaned in close to Faith and said in a

soft voice, "'Little girl, little girl, where have you been? Gathering roses to give to the Queen.'"

Suddenly Faith felt dizzy, unable to remain steady on her feet. The reporter took Faith's arm and held on tight, whispering nonsense as she walked to the window, where a row of plastic chairs had been positioned. The window behind those chairs looked out over the parking lot. They both sat, and the reporter's grip on Faith's arm remained firm.

All Faith could see of the lobby were fuzzy shapes in shades of gray. The room tilted and turned. The reporter's soft words were hollow noise. They echoed in her head until she was forced to lean forward and take her head in her hands. Still, the noise wouldn't stop. God, she wanted it to stop! Eyes closed tight, she tried to breathe. And couldn't.

She was moments away from passing out, and knew it. Faith Martin never fainted. Never! She hung on to consciousness, clung to reality with the last iota of strength she could muster. Was the woman beside her screaming? It certainly felt that way. No, not screaming, whispering. Whispering words that echoed and jabbed and made no sense.

Without warning, Luke was there. He knelt down, pushed the reporter aside and wrapped his fingers around Faith's wrists. The touch of his hands was real, and it gave Faith something to hang on to. Luke very gently pulled Faith's hands away from her face and looked into her eyes. Yes, she could concentrate on his face and those blue eyes and the touch of his hands and feel her reality returning. Luke was solid; he was real.

"What's wrong?" he asked gruffly.

Faith tried to answer but couldn't.

"I think she's having an attack or something. Maybe a seizure," the reporter explained.

Luke glared at the young woman. "Who are you?"

"Mitzi Chastain, reporter for the *Bozeman News*."

Luke released his grip on her wrists. "Faith?" he asked in a kinder tone of voice. "Are you okay?"

Faith reached out to lay a hand on his shoulder. Luke was solid and warm, and she needed that now. Colors and shapes began to return; her head no longer pounded. "I'll be fine."

"Of course you will," he assured her. He turned his head. "Michael Franklin!"

The deputy's head snapped up. "What?" he asked sleepily.

"If you can't stay awake on the job," Luke practically yelled, "then call someone in to relieve you!"

Michael yawned. "There isn't anyone to call, Luke. We're all working double shifts."

Luke cursed, then took Faith's hand and helped her to her feet. Apparently that hand was not enough, so he slipped his arm around her waist.

Faith usually shied away from assistance of any kind. She didn't lean on anyone, not ever. But right now she took great comfort in Luke's support. She was acutely aware of his strength, his height and the way he towered over her. She felt weak and small in comparison, but she also felt protected, sheltered.

It was nice. She relaxed and let herself fall against him.

No! She stiffened suddenly. This wasn't *nice*. It was bad. Very bad.

"Come on. I'm taking you home with me," he said.

"You are not!" she insisted.

"I am," he asserted without anger. "I want to keep

an eye on you for a while. Besides, Nelda always makes enough supper for a small army. You'll rest, you'll eat, and if I decide you're all right I'll take you to the motel later.''

She wanted to argue with him but didn't. Something was still wrong, and she knew it. Maybe it wouldn't be a bad idea to have another doctor around for a while. ''Okay.''

He supported her gently as they walked out of the clinic. As they left the building a blast of cold air slapping against her face helped Faith to feel more aware, more awake. Luke led her away from the clinic. Yes, the air was cold, much colder than it had been in D.C. when she'd left.

''What happened back there?'' Luke asked when they were well away from the clinic.

''I'm not sure,'' Faith said in a low voice. ''I agreed to answer a few questions for the reporter.'' Mitzi. She'd said her name was Mitzi.

''What did you tell her?'' Luke asked gruffly.

Faith opened her mouth to answer…and couldn't. She remembered nodding at the redhead, agreeing to answer a few questions, and then nothing. ''I can't remember,'' she confessed in a low voice.

''What do you mean you can't remember?'' Luke snapped. He held her a little more tightly as they hurried along. She saw their destination ahead. A solid log house surrounded by trees.

''You live here,'' she said softly as he assisted her up the steps and onto the porch.

''Yes.''

Luke opened the door and led Faith inside, and her senses were assaulted. The tantalizing aroma of dinner on the stove filled the air, and the warmth of the house wrapped itself around her in an almost tangible comfort. Colors—pillows and afghans and a bookshelf filled with books and knickknacks—were a stark contrast to the grays of the hospital.

In the kitchen, a baby laughed.

Weak once again, Faith weaved back and forth on her feet. Luke held on and led her to a fat green sofa that looked very welcoming at the moment. "Sit here. Don't move."

Faith was not accustomed to taking orders; she gave them. But this time, just this one time, she obeyed Luke's command.

# Four

Nelda took one look at Faith and decided she was *the one*. Luke could see it in the unnatural sparkle in the older woman's eyes. It was the first time he'd brought another woman into the house since Karen's death, but still… Did Nelda have to look so blasted happy about this newest turn of events?

His indispensable nanny and housekeeper also decided the new doctor needed to be fed. On that account, Faith did not disappoint her. Most women, especially those as slender as Faith, picked at meals like the ones Nelda prepared. Pot roast, corn, homemade bread, potatoes. Faith ate slowly and neatly, but she didn't eat like a bird. The woman must have the metabolism of a linebacker.

They all sat at the kitchen table, Nelda closest to the stove in case she needed to refill a serving platter or bowl, Faith on Luke's left. To his right, Abby sat in her high chair and fed herself mashed potatoes. Nelda had already given Abby her baby food. At least, she had tried. Lately the baby had been insisting that she could feed herself. She could, but she made such a mess of it Nelda tried to keep the process under control. She was usually unsuccessful.

Every now and then Faith stared at Abby as if she expected the kid to sprout another head at any moment.

Finally she asked, "How old is your daughter?"

"She turned a year old two weeks ago," Luke said.

"So she's walking?"

"Since ten and a half months," he said, remembering the first time he'd seen Abby toddling across the room, heading unerringly toward him.

Faith nodded, perhaps in approval. "Talking?"

"A little. Mostly she sputters nonsense only Nelda can decipher."

"If you'd pay attention, you'd know exactly what she's saying," Nelda said from her seat, and then she added proudly, "Abby is extremely advanced for her age."

Silently Luke agreed. But didn't every parent think their child was smarter and prettier than all the others? It was a fact of life.

"Dr. Martin," Nelda said with a wide smile. "Would you like more roast? There's plenty."

Faith considered the offer for a moment, and then declined.

After all, there was apple pie for dessert.

When the meal was finished, Faith offered to help Nelda with the dishes. If Nelda hadn't quickly and efficiently dismissed the notion, Luke would have. Faith needed to stay off her feet for a while longer. Whatever had happened back there, she was drained. As soon as he was assured she'd be okay, he'd drive her to the motel. Even though she smelled good, had a nice ass, drove him to distraction and looked adorable in his scrubs, he would not be tucking her in.

In the main room once again, Faith gravitated to the stone fireplace. Luke had built a fire there, shortly before dinner, as he did on the cool evenings he spent at home.

Faith held out her hands as if to absorb the heat, stared at the flickering flames as if they held some deep, dark secret.

"Maybe you should sit," Luke said.

"I'm fine," Faith insisted softly. He watched closely, waiting for her to sway. He would be there to steady her, if that happened. He would catch her if she fell.

"You didn't look fine when I found you in the lobby. Are you sure you're not coming down with something?" She assured him the virus wasn't spread person to person, but what if, in this one circumstance, she was wrong?

"I don't get sick," Faith insisted, but there was a hint of bewilderment in her voice.

"Never?"

"Never."

Everyone got sick now and then, and an epidemiologist was exposed to the deadliest, most contagious diseases. Faith had chosen a very dangerous profession.

Luke didn't press for more information, curious as he was. Abby toddled into the room and headed for him, arms uplifted and face smiling. Nelda had managed to wipe the mashed potatoes off her face and hands, and the oversize bib had kept her dress clean. She looked like an angel, all smiles and bright eyes. Luke caught his daughter and swung her up into his arms. She settled in and gave him a big kiss.

Abby was a happy child, in spite of the fact that her mother was gone. Of course, she didn't realize that her life was different from most little girls. She'd only been two months old when Karen had died. One day she would understand, and she'd ask questions Luke didn't want to answer. Ever.

"She's very pretty," Faith said without turning to look at him.

"Abby?"

"Of course, Abby." Faith posed casually before the fire, those baggy scrubs she wore draping across her slender body in a way that was undeniably sensual. She could have been a model instead of an epidemiologist, with a shape like hers, though she didn't seem to realize that she possessed a figure most women would kill for. "She looks like you."

"I guess so."

Faith glanced over her shoulder. "You guess so? Goodness, Luke, can't you see it?"

He shook his head. Oh, he could see the similar wave in Abby's hair, and yes, when he'd been a child his hair had been just as fine and pale blond. Her eyes were blue, like his. Beyond that, he didn't see what others saw when they said Abby had his chin, his nose, his mouth.

"Do you have any kids?" he asked. He suspected not, given her job and the way she traveled, but you could never tell.

Faith returned her attention to the fire and shook her head. "No. Sometimes I wish—" She stopped suddenly, took a deep breath and squared her shoulders. Her tone was much cooler, almost aloof, when she said, "Children and my career would not be compatible."

"I have a feeling you could find another job, if that's the only thing that's stopping you."

"I don't want another job," she said defensively. Again she glanced over her shoulder. "Besides," she said, her voice lower, softer, "having and raising a child requires so much I don't have."

*Like a husband.* She didn't say as much, but Luke suspected that was where her mind had taken her. "Maybe one day," he said, closing the uncomfortable subject.

"Maybe," she whispered.

Luke wanted to step forward and wrap his arms around Faith. He wanted to draw her into his embrace, here with Abby. At the end of the day, after all they'd been through and still had ahead of them, it seemed like a very good idea.

But he didn't move.

She'd fallen into bed weary and slept too long. So why was she still exhausted? Faith pulled herself up, throwing her legs over the side of the bed and stretching to awaken her muscles. They protested, as if trying to order her back beneath the covers.

Suddenly Faith remembered that she'd had the strangest dreams last night. She couldn't remember exactly what they'd been about, but they'd left her unsettled. Perhaps that was the reason she did not feel well rested. She searched the recesses of her mind for a snippet of the dream.

*A boat,* she recalled as she walked toward the bathroom of her small motel room. *Water. Fire.* She shuddered and shook off the nightmare. She no longer wanted to remember the dark place her mind had taken her to while she slept.

She hadn't had a vacation in years. Obviously she was in need of one. When this case was over, she would take a month off. She'd turn off her cell phone, or perhaps choose a vacation site so remote there was no cell signal to tempt her. Her server picked up no signal here in Rockland, which was par for the course. The places she worked were usually so remote no one possessed anything so frivolous as a cell phone. Here there was only one company who provided service, and that company wasn't hers.

Yes, when this was over she'd go somewhere quiet, somewhere so remote no one would find her, and… And then *what?* All she had was her work. Her work was her life, and without it she had nothing. Nothing at all.

Still half-asleep, she imagined taking a vacation with Luke…and shook the idea off before it could grow into something unmanageable.

Faith thought of herself as a logical person, a sensible woman. She could reason out this dilemma. Her biological clock was ticking; she'd made note of that fact shortly before being summoned to Montana. She'd rushed here and there he'd been. Luke Winston, intelligent, caring, handsome, healthy…and available. Something deep inside her, something primal that called back to her ancestors, had taken notice. In a crude way, it was like a mental elbow jab. *There you go, Faith. You want a baby? You feel that clock winding down and down and down? It's not too late. Here's the answer to all your prayers.*

In reality grumpy, possessive, overbearing Luke Winston was not the answer to anyone's prayers. He was simply a man, and available at a time when she'd been questioning her life and the decisions that had brought her to this point.

It didn't hurt that he occasionally looked at her as if he might be interested.

Knowing why she reacted to Luke the way she did

would make it easier not to react at all when she saw him today. At least, she hoped that was the case.

He'd driven her to the motel last night in his vehicle, a late-model SUV. And he'd left the SUV here for her, walking home after seeing her into the room. True, it wasn't far from the motel to his cabin. Rockland was so small she'd have no problem finding her way around during her time here. Everything was within walking distance, including the clinic and Luke's house.

But he didn't exactly live next door, either. Leaving his vehicle for her and walking home had been a nice gesture. Nice gestures from overbearing men were always suspect.

Luke had said he didn't want her walking to the clinic, expressing some concern about her episode in the lobby yesterday. At first, he'd offered to drive by and pick her up in the morning, but when she'd told him she planned to get to work before sunup, he'd tossed her the car keys and said he'd see her there. And then he'd walked away.

Perhaps he wasn't interested in her, after all. And why should he be? For goodness' sake, he was prettier than she was! She wasn't vain and never obsessed about her appearance, but it did seem foolish to dream of vacations with a man who could have any woman he wanted.

Men who could have any woman they wanted did not want Faith Martin.

Showered and dressed in her own clothes—a lightweight gray sweater and comfortable charcoal trousers—she drove Luke's SUV to the clinic. It didn't take her a full five minutes to get there. The parking lot was almost empty. Three vehicles remained; her

own staff's rental car and two that no doubt belonged
to nurses. There was no patrol car in the vicinity at
the moment. Considering how many hours the deputies had been working, it was possible the sheriff had
decreed no guard was necessary at four in the morning.

Something hit her face, a single sharp, cold sting,
as she walked briskly into the building. Snow? She
supposed it was possible. This was October in Montana, after all. Winter was not yet here, but it was
coming.

She made her way to the second floor, where Dr.
Gant still worked. When he saw her, he grinned
tiredly. "I expected you an hour ago."

"I overslept. Where are the others?"

"We've been sleeping in shifts," he explained.

She asked about the patients and received a satis-
factory report. Since she had arrived to take over here
in the lab, Larry Gant gladly followed the example of
his co-workers and went to find a bed. The members
of her team didn't bother to go to the motel, since they
were working different shifts and not one of them
wanted to be far away from the action. Once it had
been confirmed that this virus was indeed something
new, they had recovered their luggage and started
camping out here in the clinic.

That was what she should do, Faith thought as she
donned her lab coat. Claim a corner here in the clinic
and make do as long as the epidemic continued.

Then she remembered how Luke had walked in on
her when she'd been wearing nothing but a towel, and
she changed her mind.

Luke arrived at the clinic at seven-thirty, and walked in on mass confusion.

The three persistent reporters were in the lobby, drinking coffee and pestering Michael for answers to their questions. When they saw Luke, he was subjected to shouted queries.

"What about this latest development?"

"What can you tell us, Dr. Winston?"

"Will the town be quarantined?"

A very upset Michael placed himself between Luke and the reporters, so Luke could get onto the elevator unmolested.

What had happened? And why hadn't Faith called him?

The second floor was in chaos. A normally stoic Molly was crying. Sheriff Talbot argued heatedly with one of Faith's co-workers, Dr. White, and looked as if he wanted to break the smaller man in half.

When Molly saw Luke, she rushed toward him, wiping away her tears as she ran. "Thank goodness you're here."

He knew without being told that there was another case of the mysterious disease. "What happened?"

She didn't get a chance to answer. Sheriff Talbot turned his anger toward Luke. "Son of a bitch!" he shouted. "What the hell happened?"

"I have no idea," Luke said calmly. "Molly?"

Again Molly did not get a chance to respond. "Deputy Tyler Morris," Talbot snapped.

Luke remembered Morris. He was twenty-one and looked seventeen. Reddish blond hair, pale skin, skinny…his father was a rancher, but Tyler had dreamed of bigger and better things. Like being a Carson County deputy. "What about him?"

"His wife called me this morning, said he had a bad fever and asked what she should do. I could tell she was scared." The sheriff dragged a hand through his thinning hair. "While we were on the phone, Tyler started having convulsions. I drove over to his house and picked him up, I got him here as quick as I could, and now your lady doctor tells me it might be too late! Yesterday I had Tyler out there looking for your damned dead critters. He didn't find any, but he caught this damn disease, whatever it is."

"Get every deputy who was on that duty in here ASAP," Luke ordered.

"Your lady doctor already told me to do that," the sheriff said. "They're coming."

"Her name is Dr. Martin," Luke insisted in a low-ered voice. "Not *my lady doctor*. If Tyler survives it'll be because she's here, so cut her some slack."

The sheriff nodded. Luke didn't particularly care for Talbot, but at the moment he felt bad for the man. Carson County's sheriff was in way over his head.

"Where are they?" Luke asked as the sheriff turned his back and raked his hand through his hair again. He allowed Molly to lead him to the room where Faith and one of the Bozeman nurses, the blonde, were treating Tyler Morris. A girl who looked much too young to be a wife stood silent and pale in the far corner, watching her unconscious husband with wide eyes.

Faith wore a pristine lab coat over her own clothes, her hair was pulled back as usual but was not neatly restrained. She looked as if she'd been running, cheeks flushed and a few strands of dark hair waving wildly about her face. She did not lift her head to acknowl-edge him. The patient had all her attention at the moment.

Luke stepped to the side of the bed, quietly asking the nurse to take Morris's wife outside the room and get her something to drink and make her sit down. Neither of them wanted to go, but they did.

"Thank you, Michelle," Faith said softly as the nurse walked away with an uncertain Mrs. Morris at her side.

Faith barely glanced at Luke as he joined her. "Fever 103.2. Bilateral interstitial pulmonary infiltrates and respiratory compromise. He was having convulsions when the sheriff brought him in."

"You administered the antibiotic?"

She nodded. "I hope it's not too late." He saw the frustration and the anger on her face. "I told the sheriff to have his men wear gloves and masks when they searched for the host of the disease. Obviously my instructions were ignored, at least in this case. Do you know how much contaminant this young man would have had to take into his system in order to become this afflicted in such a short period of time?"

Luke shook his head. "Not a clue."

"The contagion must have been inhaled or ingested, somehow, and in a great quantity. If it had been introduced through the skin I don't think it could possibly have taken effect so quickly. Were any of the others this ill when they first came in?"

Luke shook his head. "No."

He felt a rush of anger himself. Defending Faith to Talbot was one thing, but he had a bone of his own to pick with her. "Why the hell didn't you call me? I don't care who you are, I don't care who sent you. This is still my clinic and these are my patients. I don't appreciate being left in the dark. I don't appreciate arriving and not knowing there's been a crisis in my own clinic. In the future I would appreciate it if you could *bother* to keep me advised when there's a significant development.''

Faith remained calm. ''Are you finished, Dr. Winston?''

He took a deep breath. ''Yes.'' Great, he had become Dr. Winston again. Still, he was certainly justified....

''You're sure you don't have anything else to say?''

''No, that's it.''

''Good.'' She looked him in the eye. ''Molly called your house immediately. Nelda said you'd already left. I'm sure she would have called you on your cell phone if she had thought it would make a significant difference in your arrival time. She did have her hands full, during those first busy minutes, as did I.''

Great, now he was a world-class jerk. ''Sorry, I should have known.''

''Yes,'' she said, ''you should have.'' She turned as if to leave the room.

''Faith,'' Luke said. ''Dr. Martin...''

She stopped before she reached the door and turned to face him. There was no more warmth in her eyes, none of the vulnerability he had seen last night. ''Yes?'' she prodded when he hesitated.

''What now?''

''Doctors White and Gant will continue to study the blood and tissue samples we've taken thus far, and Dr. Helm will assist the nurses in patient care. I can't stress strongly enough how important accurate documentation of their recovery or rejection of the antibiotic is to our research of this new disease.''

''And what are you going to do?''

She stiffened, more than a little. ''Yesterday I sent

unprepared personnel into the field to collect data. That was a mistake. As soon as all the deputies who participated in the search have received a proper dose of antibiotic, as a precautionary measure, I'm going to examine the homes and workplaces Deputy Morris visited yesterday.''

"You are not!" Luke insisted before he had a chance to think about what was coming out of his mouth.

Faith's finely shaped eyebrows raised gently. "Excuse me?"

"It's not safe," he argued in a calmer voice.

"This is my responsibility, Luke," she said, finally reverting to her use of his given name. "I'm certainly more prepared for the task than this boy was. I should have done that job myself, instead of sending civilians to search for something they don't understand."

"Mice and birds," Luke snapped. "What's not to understand?"

"I don't know," Faith confessed.

Luke glanced back at the deputy on the hospital bed. Faith was right. Deputy Morris was a boy. "Is he going to make it?"

"I can't say just yet," Faith said pragmatically, and then she turned away too quickly.

Luke followed her. "Wait." He caught up with her easily. "Are you really going into the field to ferret out this contagion by yourself?"

"Yes," she said, so sternly he knew she was gearing up for a fight.

Luke did not argue with her, not this time. "I'm going with you."

# Five

Faith couldn't imagine why Luke had insisted on coming along, but she said nothing to dissuade him. He was very proprietary about his patients and his town, and had been since her arrival, so she supposed he wanted to be involved in all aspects of the investigation.

Besides, she had a feeling they could argue all morning on this point and she would not win.

He drove her to the house where Angela Carter and her son Benjy, both patients in the Carson County Clinic, resided. It was one of the homes Tyler Morris had examined yesterday. Faith was determined. If she didn't find anything here, she'd move on to another house the deputy had examined. If it took all day, all night, all week, she would find the source of the virus the media called Rockland Fever.

Again Faith saw spitting icy flakes. They pelted Luke's windshield at irregular intervals, not enough to call a snow shower but a definite sign that winter was coming. The temperature was rising slowly, and it would soon be a few degrees too warm for snow, but what about tonight and tomorrow night? This would not be a quickly solved case; she could very well be here for weeks. Once the antigen was isolated and they knew if the development of a cure or a vaccine was possible, she would like to take her time and examine all the patients more carefully. She wanted to follow their progress as they recovered. It wasn't every day that a new and lethal virus surfaced.

The sheriff followed in his own patrol car. Talbot had been every bit as insistent about the matter as Luke had been. She could have told them both that she didn't need assistance, but neither of them would have listened to her. Men.

Faith felt more confident of winning an argument with the sheriff than with Luke. Something about the small-town doctor made her struggle to maintain her usual composed demeanor.

When she and Luke went inside the Carter house, each of them properly outfitted in protective gear that covered them from head to toe, she insisted that the lawman remain behind. Sheriff Talbot did not argue with her. Perhaps he was more intelligent than he appeared at first glance.

Angela Carter was a single mother, a widow Luke said, who lived in a small, neat house with her young son. At the front door Faith began a systematic search. Now and then she glanced at Luke, who seemed to be doing nothing more than watching her. If that was his only purpose in coming along, he'd wasted his time. She didn't need a watchdog, and she never had. For as long as she could remember, she had been able to take care of herself.

For as long as she could remember.

After a few awkward moments, she dismissed Luke Winston and threw herself into the examination of the house. The only clutter was the occasional baby toy that had been deposited by a chair or under a table. There was no evidence of a rodent invasion, no birds—domestic or wild—inside or outside the house.

As Faith mentally dismissed her audience and threw herself into the search for the contagion that had affected the entire county, the pieces of this maddening puzzle began to drift and twist and rearrange.

She was missing something. Something important. Never in her life had she confronted a case so infuriating. Science made sense in every way. It was logical. The answers were always right there, waiting to be discovered. Why was *this* puzzle so difficult?

When she had been through the small house twice, she returned to the kitchen and placed herself in the center of the room. She closed her eyes and concentrated on the complete silence that filled the house, and she let her mind go.

Her mind was the one thing she could depend on, no matter what. Everything, *everything,* could be explained rationally. There was a discovery waiting to be made, and she was close. So close. She recalled in great detail everything she had seen in the makeshift laboratory in Luke's clinic. Every blood sample, every tissue sample. The physical reaction of every patient to the antibiotic she had administered. There was a source for the virus, an end to the epidemic, and it was here in this house. Somewhere, somehow, it was *here*.

Luke was here, too. She was aware of his presence, and yet he did not disturb her. He remained quiet and motionless, and he waited on the opposite side of the room, as if he knew he would disturb her if he stood too close. For a moment, just a moment, she was vaguely distracted, as if a butterfly flitted and danced in her peripheral vision. Yes, she did feel something awkward and unexpected for Luke Winston, but it wasn't real. She had fabricated a spark, a trill of passion, because she'd been thinking of babies lately.

That was all, that was the explanation. What she felt wasn't real. It couldn't be.

Her eyes flew open. *Not real.* "It's not organic," she whispered.

"What?" Luke took a step toward her.

She looked at him, the revelation that had just come to her making her heart pound furiously. "The source of the virus," she said breathlessly. "It was manufactured. That's why the deputies didn't find any evidence of diseased mice or birds in the patients' homes. The virus was manufactured in a laboratory."

"How can you be sure?" Luke asked, his gloved hands flexing, the eyes beyond the mask growing hard. She couldn't blame him for being upset. An epidemic was a disaster, but it was a natural disaster. What would bring bioterrorism to Carson County?

"There was always something about the samples I studied that didn't ring true," Faith said, excitement making her voice just a touch too loud. "The fact that so many were affected at once, that they lived miles apart, that the symptoms were exactly the same in all cases." She began to glance around the kitchen. She would have to search the house again, and this time…she had no idea what she was looking for. How would such a virus be delivered? Different neighborhoods had been affected, all at approximately the same time. With a new virus, those first afflicted usually trickled in one at a time over a period of weeks, even months. Luke had had twenty-two patients in a span of four days.

Her search quickly took her to a stack of mail on the kitchen table. The stack had been disturbed, which, if she were correct, explained Tyler Morris's affliction.

She found the offending envelope, an advertisement

for a vacation resort in Florida. When she very carefully removed the slick flyer, a single page featuring an appealing photograph of turquoise water and white sand, a small amount of greenish-yellow powder drifted to the table.

Faith turned her head to stare at Luke, and for the first time she was really and truly glad that he was here, that she was not alone.

Her voice remained soft as she told him, "The homes and workplaces of your patients must be evacuated and cordoned off immediately. Anyone who's been in an affected area must be brought into the clinic for treatment." Her heart pounded too hard. "Luke, we don't know how many of these time bombs are out there." She imagined mail left unopened, or disposed of improperly, that greenish-yellow powder just waiting to be inhaled.

"I'll talk to the sheriff," Luke said.

"He's going to need help," Faith said as they walked toward the front door. "I'll make a few phone calls."

They stepped onto the front porch, and Sheriff Talbot moved anxiously forward.

Faith drew her mask down and off. "Effective immediately, this town is quarantined."

Luke had thought his life and his town hectic before, but things very quickly got worse.

Bioterrorism. It was not a word he had ever expected to hear in relation to Carson County. The National Guard had arrived within hours of Faith's phone call, along with two government officials who set up shop in an abandoned building half a mile from the clinic. The State Patrol blocked the roads out of town, and military helicopters occasionally flew overhead. Their job was to keep people out of Carson County; and more important, to keep the virus in.

A haz-mat team would soon arrive to sweep the area and contain the contaminant. Every last grain had to be found.

What had been news became big news. Since the area was quarantined, the three reporters who had remained in town after the initial wave of interest were getting exclusive stories. Since they weren't going anywhere anytime soon, they communicated by phone, fax and laptop. By afternoon the news was on every channel, along with an old photo of Faith and a snapshot of Luke that someone had dug up.

The resort advertised in the mailing Faith had found did not exist. The only fingerprints found on the envelopes and the slick ads had belonged to the victims who were dead or ailing. Postmarks revealed that the mailings had been made from a Tampa, Florida post office over a period of four days, which accounted for the timing of the appearance of symptoms. The FBI would continue to investigate, but Luke suspected that investigation would take them nowhere.

Three unopened envelopes had been found, by lucky people who had either been out of town or who had a bad habit of letting their mail sit for days at a time.

One other deputy became ill, but he did not become as sick as Tyler Morris. Faith treated and admitted him. The clinic, which had been overcrowded since this epidemic began, was filled to overflowing. Soldiers, deputies, patients, doctors…you couldn't turn around without running into someone. Sometimes literally.

Benjy was moved into Angela's room, and they were both better for it.

Faith worked nonstop, as dedicated as he'd ever seen any woman. Or any man. She was organized, she was efficient. And man, did she know how to take charge. At the moment, this was her clinic and her people, and he didn't mind at all. She was a wonder to watch.

Not that he had much time to watch her, or anything else.

Other people in Carson County continued to suffer from ordinary illnesses and accidents. For the past week, Luke had been able to treat them over the phone or via Molly, but some things could not be put off. Danny Mann broke his finger, and Lydia Potter's cough—just an everyday annoying cough, thank God—was getting worse. No one wanted to enter the clinic, not when it was filled with very sick people and heavily guarded by armed men.

Luke set up a makeshift clinic in a vacant building two blocks down from the Carson County Clinic. Molly assisted, leaving the Bozeman nurses and their own Betsy to work at the clinic with Faith and her team. Together he and Molly managed to see a dozen patients in the temporary clinic. He would never have thought an afternoon like this to be calming, but it was nice to get back into something resembling a routine.

Though he told his patients that all would be well, they were scared, and rightly so. Luke assured them wholeheartedly and honestly, knowing Faith was doing her best. He could sincerely tell his patients that the town was in the best of hands.

When the last patient had been seen, he and Molly locked the front door of their temporary clinic. He'd set a broken finger and prescribed cough syrup and antibiotics and a cream for Joe Peterson's persistent rash. He'd listened to a dozen heartbeats and listened to frightened concerns about what was to come. His day had been tame, he knew, compared to what Faith had likely been through. He did not envy her, reliving this scenario again and again. But that was her job— assisting in the fight of one epidemic after another.

He and Molly walked toward the clinic. For a few moments, they said nothing. Their minds were in the same place, though.

"Think we'll make it, Luke?" Molly asked.

"Of course we will."

She snorted, as if she saw right through his outward confidence and discovered the hidden doubts. "I keep thinking about this movie I saw once, where a bunch of people got sick and no one knew what the disease was. It turned out to be created in a lab, just like this one. In the end it killed everyone. Well, almost everyone. The star survived. I think there was a sequel, but it was pretty bad. Anyway, the important point is, everyone but the movie star died."

"That's fiction, Molly. Fiction," Luke said.

"Yeah, but they say truth is stranger than fiction, and I'm beginning to believe it."

She had a point. Why on earth would anyone want to attack here? There were no military facilities anywhere near Carson County. The only government here was that of a small county and an insignificant town. There was no logical reason for them to be attacked.

As they reached the clinic, Molly headed for the entrance. Luke caught her arm. "Go on home," he said. "You haven't left this place in days."

"I took a couple of hours yesterday." Molly

brushed a strand of wind-blown hair away from her face. "I'm fine."

None of them was fine, but Luke didn't share that observation with his nurse. "Sleep in your own bed, hug Harry, eat something sitting down..."

"Later," she said, reaching for the door and brushing past a very young private who recognized both Molly and Luke and let them enter the building without question.

"Tonight," Luke insisted. "I want you to go home tonight for at least eight hours."

As they stepped onto the elevator, Molly gave him a grim smile. "After you, chief."

Faith had spent most of the afternoon studying the lethal powder they'd found in Angela Carter's home, and in many others. Fortunately her antibiotic was an effective treatment, as long as the infected person received it soon enough. Deputy Morris was stable though not as improved as she'd like, but the others were doing well.

As long as there were no more cases, they'd be fine. Of course, the hazardous materials team that had arrived with the military would search every home and business in the county, to make sure there were no more envelopes of this contagion out there, waiting to be inhaled or handled with unprotected hands.

She kept the virulent powder in a Plexiglas container, wore protective gear at all times, and had chased everyone from the lab hours ago. Here in the lab she could ignore the melee that was going on all around her and concentrate on her job. Now that she had the virus in substantial form to study, she should quickly be able to discover if a vaccine or an outright cure was possible.

She tried to tune out everything, but in the back of her mind she worried about the people here. Rockland and the rest of Carson County would never be the same.

When the door to the lab opened, Faith snapped her head around. Molly barely peeked in. "You have a phone call."

"From whom?"

"A man. Said his name was…" Molly hesitated as she tried to recall the name. "Jake Ingram," she finally said quickly.

"Never heard of him," Faith snapped. "Take a message."

Molly shook her head. "I tried. He says it's urgent."

"Take a number and I'll call him back."

"Tried that, too. He says it's a matter of life and death."

Every day of her life presented her with a matter of life and death! "Fine." Faith began to strip off her protective gear as she walked away from her work area.

While she scrubbed at the sink on the far side of the room, Molly said, "Take it in Luke's office. It'll be quiet there and you can sit down. I'll bring you something to eat and a cold drink."

"Thanks." Faith walked toward the door. "I won't be there that long."

The armed guard at the door, illogically dressed in jungle camo and wearing a helmet, nodded at her as she passed. Faith returned the gesture. At least she didn't have to worry about anyone disturbing her work while she was away from the lab to answer this supposedly urgent phone call.

Faith sat down in Luke's padded swivel chair. It was nice to sit, she grudgingly admitted as she lifted the receiver to her ear. "Faith Martin," she said crisply.

There was a moment of silence. She almost hung up the phone. A split second before she pulled the phone from her ear, a deep voice said, "Faith?"

"Speaking. Who is this and what do you want? I have a crisis here. I'm told this is a life-and-death emergency. If it's not—"

"It is," the voice on the phone assured her. "My name is Jake Ingram."

"So I've been told. What's the emergency, Mr. Ingram?"

"I saw your photograph on the news."

Faith closed her eyes for a long moment. Jake Ingram, if that was indeed his real name, was a nut. A nutcase who had seen her on the news and had tracked her down. Great. Now she'd have to have someone screen her calls. "Mr. Ingram—" She stopped speaking when the door opened and Molly walked in, a cold soda in one hand, a granola bar in the other. Faith had said she wasn't hungry, but suddenly she was eternally grateful to Luke's nurse, who placed the offerings on the desk and stepped quietly out of the room. "You have ten seconds," she said as she reached for the soda.

"That's not enough time," the man said, clearly agitated. "There's so much to explain. I have so much to tell you."

"Goodbye, Mr. Ingram. Don't call again." Faith was moving the phone away from her ear, intent on hanging up on the man, when his voice rang through the phone.

"Do you remember anything of your life before the age of ten?"

Faith's heart almost stopped. She slowly brought the phone back to her ear. "What did you say?" she asked softly.

In a matter of minutes, Jake Ingram told her a fantastic story, and she listened. The story was preposterous, unbelievable...and yet she did not hang up on him.

He told her briefly and succinctly of a secret scientific experiment, success, betrayal and death.

Certain words and phrases rang oddly true, though Faith found no memory of the time Jake Ingram spoke about. In a few instances she experienced a chill that cut to her very bones. Mark. Gideon. Brothers with whom she'd supposedly shared a womb. Grace, a sister. Jake, an overly protective big brother. As Jake told her of a harrowing escape, the dream of a few nights ago came back to her. Water. Fire. A sense of loss she could not explain.

What followed was a warning she could not accept. Jake Ingram said she and the others had received hypnotic programming that should not be possible, not now and certainly not then.

According to this man, she was one of the super-babies she'd read about in the supermarket tabloids— Proteans, some called them, after the name of the research project, Code Proteus, that supposedly created them. He referred to her as a ticking time bomb, just waiting for the delivery of a trigger that would force her to do something evil for the organization Jake Ingram called the Coalition.

Being logical, Faith quickly found a way to dismiss the man's story. He'd seen her on the news, and for some reason had done a background check. How hard would it have been to discover that she'd been adopted at the age of ten? The rest of the story was fantasy, a sick man's way to torture her with the past she had never been able to recall.

"I didn't want to tell you over the phone," Ingram said in an almost kind voice. "But since the town is quarantined and I can't get in, I had no choice. Faith, you're in danger. The Coalition I mentioned earlier, they want you. They want to get their hands on you before you're deprogrammed. We can't allow that to happen."

Suddenly Faith had a headache. Her head swam. She quickly convinced herself the reaction was caused by hunger, nothing more. She reached for the soda and took a sip.

"This is the most ridiculous story—"

"It's far-fetched, I know, but not ridiculous," Ingram insisted. "Faith, you have to get out of there. If I found you, so will the Coalition. They want—"

"What do *you* want?" she snapped.

"I want you safe," he said, sounding sincere. Obviously the man was an accomplished actor. "Please, let me arrange for you to be transported out of Carson County and taken to a safe place."

"Impossible." Like she would actually let this man take her anywhere!

"Mark is dying to see you."

Again her heart flipped and fluttered. "I don't know anyone named Mark."

"You do," Jake said softly. "Reach back, Faith. Remember."

She panicked and slammed the phone down, abruptly ending the phone call.

Before she left the room, the phone began to ring again. Faith ignored it as she slammed the door behind her and returned to the lab. She tried to dismiss the man's words, but she couldn't. What he said was impossible. Ridiculous. So why did her heart continue to flutter? Why did she have to push away the memories of last night's harrowing dream?

Because she was tired, that was why. This had been the most bizarre trip! First her unexpected attraction to Luke, and now this.

Before she was emotionally ready for work again, the door opened and Molly stuck her head in again. "That man called back."

"I don't want to talk to him again," Faith said sharply. "If Mr. Ingram continues to call, report him to the sheriff." Let Talbot handle Ingram! She had no desire to talk to him again. Ever.

"He left a message," Molly said, holding up a scrap of paper.

Faith rolled her eyes. "Do I want to know what that message is?"

"It's a cell phone number," Molly said, reaching into the room to lay the scrap of paper on a metal table. "He said when you're ready to hear more, call him day or night. Anytime."

"Is that it?"

Molly shook her head. "He also said for me to tell you that he cares about you and only wants what's best for you."

Great. The man was not just a nutcase, he was a potential stalker. Just what she needed.

Since the town was quarantined and she had an

armed guard at her door, she didn't have to worry about Jake Ingram. Not today, at least.

But no matter how she tried, she could not get that phone call off her mind.

Finally, in a fit of anger, Faith crossed the room and snatched up the paper with Jake Ingram's phone number scribbled on it. After a moment's hesitation, she crumpled the paper in her hand and tossed it into the nearest trash can.

# Six

Luke wandered down the hall of the clinic, long after dark. There was only so much they could do tonight. The virus had been identified, and the patients were on the mend. Those who might have been exposed had been given the new antibiotic, as a precaution.

The armed guards stationed in and around his clinic, as they were stationed in and around the county, gave the place that was so familiar to him an unreal atmosphere. Luke was consumed by the certainty that this tragedy should not have happened here.

He'd finally convinced Molly to go home for a few hours. The woman was about to drop on her feet. Faith, who walked toward him with a strained and pale expression on her face, looked even worse than Luke's number one nurse.

"How about we call it a night," he said, trying to give her a half smile he did not feel.

"I can't. I have too much work to do."

"I'll feed you," he promised. "Real, hot food."

That offer elicited a short-lived smile from Faith. "Sweet-talker."

"Come on," he said when she looked as if she planned to keep on walking. She'd work through the night, if no one stopped her. "Take a couple of hours, at least."

"It has been a long day," she conceded. "Maybe I could use a break."

Luke had a suspicion that Dr. Faith Martin didn't take many breaks, that she was harder on herself than she was on anyone else. He had the urge to wrap his arms around her and protect her from all this. But he also knew she would never agree that she needed to be protected from anything.

Soldiers kept the reporters at a distance, as Luke and Faith made their escape. The redhead was particularly persistent, but this time even she fell back quickly. As she retreated, the redhead seemed to be flirting with one of the soldiers, more interested in him than in the physicians at the moment.

Nelda and Abby were already asleep, but as always, there was plenty of food in the refrigerator. All Luke had to do was heat it up. Tonight it was stew, hearty and, while it heated on the stove, aromatic.

Faith sat at the kitchen table and watched him work. As he took bowls from the cabinet, she asked abruptly, "Have you read about the genetics experiments that supposedly took place in the sixties and early seventies?"

Luke glanced over his shoulder, surprised by the question. "Sure. Hasn't everyone?"

She shook her head. "Not me. I was out of the country for months, before coming here. Africa and then India. It wasn't until I got back and saw this bizarre headline on the front page of a newspaper…" Her voice faded into nothing. After a few deep breaths, she found her voice again. "Do you think it's possible?"

Luke shrugged. Had he really hoped for more personal conversation from Faith Martin? This was shop talk.

He'd read the articles, wondered about them, and then dismissed the matter from his mind. "I guess if you think about it, anything is possible. I don't think it's probable, though."

She nodded as if she agreed. "Neither do I. It's extremely unlikely that such advances were made without the knowledge of the entire medical community. Have you ever heard of a man named Jake Ingram?"

Talk about an abrupt change in subject! Luke had to think for a moment before answering, "Sure. Ingram is some rich guy from...Texas? I think Texas. He's a financial wizard, or something like that."

Faith looked surprised. "Rich? Are you sure? There's probably more than one man named Jake Ingram," she suggested.

"Probably." Luke carried two steaming bowls of stew to the table and sat. "How do you know him?" he asked.

"I don't, not really," Faith said.

Great. If he did decide to take a chance and pursue his attraction to Faith, what chance did he have? She wasn't going to be here much longer, and even if she was, of course other men were interested in her. How could he hold a candle to some rich hotshot?

"The children," Faith said abruptly, again changing the subject without warning. She played with her stew rather than eating it. "If the stories are true and there are genetically altered children, they'd be freaks, wouldn't they?" She stirred the stew and lifted a spoonful only to let it dribble back into the bowl.

"Freaks is a strong word," Luke said.

"But they would be *different,*" she insisted. "Not…normal."

"What's normal?" Luke asked. He intended his question as a lighthearted joke, but Faith didn't take it as such. She shook her head and closed her eyes.

"Eat," he commanded. "And then you can stay here for the night."

Her eyes got wide.

"You can sleep on the couch," he clarified.

The shock faded from her face, but still she shook her head. "I'd prefer to return to the motel. I…I need to be alone."

She needed to be alone. Suddenly Luke realized he was damned tired of being alone. He had Abby, sure, but that wasn't enough. Not anymore. Maybe that was why he found Faith so damned attractive, so appealing; maybe that was why she had worked her way under his skin. He wanted her to spend the night, but he damn sure didn't want her sleeping on the couch.

He wondered if Faith was capable of carrying on a casual conversation. No shop talk, no questions about other men, no far-fetched medical suppositions.

There was only one way to find out. "So," he said as he lifted a spoonful of stew. "What do you like to do when you're not chasing down viruses?"

Faith looked mildly shocked. "I beg your pardon?"

"Hobbies, entertainment, peccadilloes," he explained. "What do you do in your spare time?"

Her dark blue eyes were impossibly wide. "I don't have any spare time."

Luke laughed. "Everyone has spare time, Faith. Come on, throw me a bone here. Tell me what you're like when you're not no-nonsense Dr. Martin."

"Why?" she asked seriously.

He had never had so much trouble getting a woman to talk about herself. Maybe it wasn't worth the trouble, trying to get to know Faith. Then again...

"I'm interested," he said. *Interested* could mean so many things.

Faith was stumped. Genuinely taken aback. Finally she said, "Oh! I like to read."

It was a start. "Mysteries? Romance? Creepy horror novels?"

Did she look sheepish? "Medical manuals and periodicals, primarily, though I am also interested in travelogues."

Medicine was her job, and she traveled all the time, from what he'd been able to tell. "Surely there's—"

"What about you?" Faith interrupted. "What are your hobbies?" She looked at him as if she were certain he didn't have any, either.

"Trout fishing is my favorite," he said. "But I also like to kayak and golf when I can. I tried skiing once, but I busted my ass and decided the sport wasn't for me. Living that dangerously isn't my style."

"Oh," she said softly.

"I do like to hike, but I haven't done that in a while, and there are lots of places near here to go horseback riding, but I don't do that often, either."

"When do you have time to see patients?" she asked dryly.

"I manage."

She gave the stew her full attention.

"When this is all over, I'll show you a part of Montana you don't see from the clinic," Luke promised.

Faith glanced at him almost warily. "Oh, you will?"

"I'll take you fishing first, see how you like the

great outdoors. If you survive the fishing expedition, then we'll see about the kayaking.''

''If I survive?'' Faith asked with a widening smile. ''I had no idea trout fishing could be considered such a challenge.''

''We could always try something less ambitious first. A walk in the woods, maybe.''

''Why on earth would I want to walk in the woods?'' she asked.

It took a minute for Luke to realize that she was serious. Completely, cluelessly serious. ''Because it's beautiful,'' he said. *And because I'd love to get you away from the clinic and under the trees and kiss you until your head swam.*

Fat chance.

''Late in the spring, there's a festival right here in Rockland,'' he said, attempting to veer his mind away from the walk in the woods he would never experience. ''It's really lots of fun. There's a craft fair, a pie-eating contest and a dance, among other things.''

''I don't dance,'' Faith said with a wide smile, ''and I certainly wouldn't have anything to contribute to the craft fair. But I might be interested in entering a pie-eating contest.''

''I'll teach you to dance,'' Luke suggested in an offhand manner.

Faith's smile died and she stiffened just slightly. ''This is lovely dinner conversation, but of course, I won't be here in the spring.''

''Of course not,'' Luke agreed.

There was no telling where Faith Martin would be come spring. Across the world and up to her elbows in something nasty, most likely.

Too bad. He really would like to get the chance to

teach her to fish. To walk in the woods. To dance. But Faith was all business, and that would never happen.

Faith had been tempted to take Luke up on his offer and sleep on his couch. His house was warm, secure, and even though she had insisted that she wanted to be alone tonight, it was a lie. It would be nice to know there was someone in the next room, a friend she could call on if she were bothered by nightmares again, a friendly face to look at over breakfast.

But staying at his place was not a good idea. Especially once he started talking about Rockland in the spring, dancing at a town festival and walking in the woods. She didn't have that kind of life and she never would. She didn't even long for such ordinary things. A twitch of her nose and an unsettled clenching in her stomach protested her silent insistence, but she didn't back down. No, she did not yearn for such simple pleasures.

Though during the day she'd seen spitting snow more than once, the night was cold but clear. The moon shone bright in a black sky that was free of clouds at the moment. Luke had insisted on driving her to the motel, even though she could have walked to the clinic and caught a ride from a soldier or even walked directly to the motel. It wasn't that far.

The short ride was silent, a little bit uncomfortable. She felt as if she should say something.

But what?

In her entire thirty-three years, Faith had been a part of two relationships that might be called, by some, romantic. Both partners had been doctors who worked in her field, and both had entered her life as friends first.

Once romance had been introduced to the mix, things had quickly gone wrong. Faith was uncomfortable with the expectations involved in such a relationship. Her own, and those of her partner. Early in her twenties, she'd occasionally dreamed of finding a love and passion that made the rest of the world seem insignificant, in spite of the fact that she herself was not a great beauty and never would be.

Her two disastrous so-called romances had taught her to put aside her dreams. She would not change who she was to please a man, set aside her career for his, become second best because it was what he expected of her. That seemed to be what was required to keep a man happy.

Neither of the men she'd been involved with had ever made her shiver when she looked at them, the way she sometimes did when she laid her eyes on Luke. Yes, he was handsome, but her reaction to him went deeper than an admiration for his obvious beauty.

There had been such a sparkle in his eyes when he'd talked about teaching her to fish. And when he'd said he'd teach her to dance.

Her one attempt at learning to dance had been a disaster. She'd been seventeen at the time, and so worried about each and every move that she'd become confused and tripped over her own feet. The idea of dancing with Luke was interesting, even though she knew it was impossible. He would never hold her close and guide her across a smooth dance floor while whispering in her ear. But if he did, when he whispered he would say—

Heaven above! She was apparently as foolish today as she'd been when she'd been young and silly enough to believe in great love and passion. Again she wrote

her response to Dr. Winston off to her relentlessly
ticking biological clock.

No, that clock no longer ticked. It pounded. Each
second roared past.

Luke pulled into a parking space at her door, put
the SUV into park and turned to look at her. "I'll pick
you up in the morning."

"That's not necessary," Faith said, dismissing her
daydreams. "I will probably go in very early again.
I'll call the clinic and have…"

"I don't care what time you plan to get to work,
I'm going to pick you up and we're going in together."

She gave in too easily. "Okay. Pick me up at four."

He didn't look too terribly stunned, but there was a
telling lift to his eyebrows. "A.m.?"

She smiled. "It's not too late to back out."

"No way. Four a.m. it is."

Faith laid her hand on the door handle, but before
she could open the door Luke stopped her with his
hand on her shoulder. "I don't think I ever thanked
you for everything you've done since you came here."

She glanced back. "You did."

"Not enough. Without your new antibiotic, there
would be more infected people laid up right now, and
there's no telling how many of my patients would be
dead. Benjy and Tyler, without doubt, would be gone.
Others too, I'm sure."

"I was just doing my job."

"You're damn good at what you do," he said. "I
might not have greeted you warmly when you first
arrived, but, Faith…I'm very glad you're here."

Luke didn't drop his hand from her shoulder and
say good-night. He leaned toward her, slowly. Gently.

"I'm going to kiss you," he said as he moved slowly nearer. "If you want me to stop, now's the time to speak up."

Faith held her breath. Why would Luke want to kiss her? As a way of conveying his thanks? No. That wasn't it. She saw the expression in his eyes; he'd looked very much this way when he'd talked about fishing. His interest in kissing her had nothing to do with the virus that had brought her to Carson County. Judging by his eyes and the set of his mouth and the tension in his neck, his interest mirrored her impossibly unrealistic daydreams.

Moving away, saying good-night and jumping out of the car before his mouth touched hers would be the wisest course of action. Faith always, *always,* took the wisest course of action.

So why didn't she move away?

Luke's mouth was soft and warm, and he barely brushed it against hers. Faith held her breath as the sensation of his lips on hers shook her to her very core. Her body's response to something so simple—a brush of lip, the faintest impression of tongue—surprised her.

No, it rattled her. She wanted to grab Luke and hang on tight, deepen the kiss, ask for more.

If she invited him to come inside with her, would he say yes? Of course he would. If she expressed an interest in taking him into her bed, would he consent? Almost certainly. Perhaps one evening with Luke in her bed would put an end to the unexpected demands of her traitorous body.

"Good-night," she said quickly, throwing the door open and stepping into the cold parking lot.

"See you in the morning," Luke said, apparently not at all affected by the brief kiss.

She let herself into her room, her fingers fumbling slightly as she inserted the key into the lock. Luke didn't pull away until she was inside with the door locked behind her.

Faith got ready for bed calmly and rather quickly, her mind on everything but the simple nightly rituals. When she climbed into bed, her short cotton pajamas much too lightweight for the cool Montana night but comfortable in the warm room, her mind did not stop spinning.

The virus and all the questions still attached.

The phone call from Jake Ingram.

Luke and the way he kissed.

Fishing.

She could do nothing about the first two dilemmas. The virus would be waiting for her in the morning, and as for the phone call, she had almost completely dismissed it as a prank of some kind. If she had the time, she'd research this Jake Ingram and the stories about the genetically engineered children.

But not tonight. She was tired. Exhausted, really. Much more drained than she should be. Any energy she possessed had to be directed toward ending the epidemic in Carson County. Tonight she had no excess energy.

So she closed her eyes and thought about that kiss. Faith had always been very aware of her body. Heart rate, blood pressure, body temperature. With a minimum of effort she could monitor them all. How old had she been when she'd realized that not everyone had the same gift? Late into her teens, she supposed.

Right now, her heart rate, BP and body temp were

all slightly elevated. Not only that, something deep inside her quivered. It was a primal craving, an instinctive cry.

She wanted Luke, in a way she had never wanted another man. She wanted him to hold her, kiss her again, part her thighs and fill her. Just the imagining made her quiver.

If she were a bold woman, she would call Luke right now. She would ask him to come back to her. Now. Quickly. *Touch me.*

And he would say yes.

Faith didn't reach for the phone to call Luke. Of course she didn't. The days when she'd been foolish enough to even consider such an action were long behind her. She set her mental clock, the only alarm she ever needed, for three-forty and drifted into a restless sleep.

Luke stood beside Abby's crib, staring down at his sleeping daughter. She was so beautiful. So pure and good. She was also the light of his life, the only thing that had kept him on his feet and functioning for the past ten months.

He should be asleep, but his mind wouldn't rest.

For ten months he had blamed himself for Karen's death and mentally prepared himself to live the rest of his life alone. The guilt he'd felt when he'd buried his wife was not gone, but it had faded to a point where he could live with himself. There were so many reasons to blame himself for everything that had happened. He hadn't loved his wife enough. If they'd been living in a bigger city with a first-class hospital, maybe Karen would be alive today.

Logically, he knew that wasn't true. The aneurysm

that had killed Karen would have killed her no matter where she'd been. She'd been dead before the sheriff had called; she'd died so quickly no one could have saved her. And still, knowing she had hated it here made him wonder, in the recesses of his mind, if maybe, just maybe…

Luke had tried to put the maybes aside so he could function. He had Abby, he had his work. He didn't need anything else. That was how he'd survived to this point. Numb. Going through life like a robot.

In a matter of days, Faith had changed that. God help him, he wanted her so bad he ached with it. He had taken that kiss tonight, knowing it was wrong, knowing he could ruin a budding friendship, knowing nothing could come of what he felt for her. One kiss, he'd told himself. One quick, passionless kiss.

The kiss had been quick, but it had not been passionless. It had taken every ounce of strength he had to keep his hands off her, and quiet and still as Faith had been, he'd seen and felt the deep response in her. She wouldn't have run from him so quickly if she hadn't felt some of what he did. The kiss had scared her.

Nothing could come of this. Faith was a highly respected epidemiologist who traveled almost constantly. She was intelligent and beautiful and driven, and if she wanted a man she could certainly have her pick.

Luke was a country doctor who liked his life as it was, or had until Faith had arrived to turn everything upside down. What did they have? Nothing. There was no middle ground, no grand possibilities, no hope for a future of any kind.

But they had today, didn't they? And tomorrow.

And maybe a few more days after that. It wasn't enough, but if it was all he could have he'd take it.

He had thanked Faith for saving the lives of so many of his patients, and she seemed uncomfortable with his genuine and perfectly understandable gratitude. How could he ever thank her for waking him from his long, dark sleep? Thanks to Faith, Luke finally realized that he was still alive. He hadn't buried his hopes with Karen; he hadn't died with her.

He could live again, and he could laugh. He could appreciate the simple power of a kiss, savor the sensation of a woman's soft skin beneath his fingers. Like any man, he could hunger for a woman's touch.

And maybe, just maybe, he could love again.

# Seven

Faith was scared. So scared. Her heart was beating a hundred and twenty beats per minute, she had begun to sweat and she couldn't breathe deeply. No matter how she tried, she could not take a deep breath.

She was frightened and confused and running for her life, and she was ten years old again.

There were five of them…and then there were four. Where was Gideon? Faith's heart began to pound. She was lost in darkness, but at least she wasn't alone. Run. Hide. Stick together, now and forever. She couldn't see, but she could hear the frantic footsteps of her siblings. She could not see their faces, she did not know their names, but she knew they were a part of her. They were family.

A loud noise, a flash of light, flames, and suddenly Faith was no longer running; she was drowning. Water filled her lungs, a strong current dragged her down, and there was a bone-chilling darkness. *I'm going to die.*

Just when she thought there was no hope, strong arms captured her, steadied her and pulled her to the surface. She knew, with a surge of hope, who had saved her in her darkest moment. It was Mark who dragged her from the depths of the ocean and into the light. Mark. Her brother.

"Faith!" Mark cried. She almost saw his face,

through her tears and the salt water in her eyes, but
he remained an elusive figure. "Breathe. Please
breathe."

She blinked, and his face became more defined…but his features were not crisp enough to suit
her. They faded and blurred in the most frustrating
way. She wanted to see Mark so badly. More than that,
she *needed* to see his face. He had the brightest
smile….

"Dammit, Faith!"

The sharp words dragged her clumsily and quickly
into the world of the waking. The dream was gone in
an instant, and as soon as her eyes were open, she
began to forget. For a moment she tried to hang on to
that feeling of belonging that had cut through the fear,
but it all faded, as she looked up and directly into
Luke's worried face.

He sat on the side of her bed, one hand still gripping
her arm too tightly.

"What are you doing here?" she asked, shaking off
what remained of the dream.

"I came by to pick you up," he explained, "as
planned." A muscle in Luke's jaw twitched; his neck
corded with tension. He abruptly released her arm. "I
pounded on the door for several minutes, but you
didn't answer. I got worried so I called your room on
my cell phone. When you didn't pick up, I phoned the
clinic to see if you were there. When Dr. Helm said
he hadn't seen you since you left last night, I panicked."

Faith glanced at the bedside table. Not only had her
internal alarm clock failed her, but she'd slept deeply
while the phone not two feet from her head rang.
"How did you get into my room?"

"I woke up Eugene, the motel manager," Luke explained. "He's the one who let me in." Suddenly the man hovering above her looked less anxious and more than a little sheepish. "It was either that or break down the door."

"I can't believe I was sleeping so deeply," Faith said. She realized that her gown was twisted—and too thin to wear in mixed company—so she pulled the bedcover to her chest.

Faith had never had a man sit on the edge of her bed as she came awake. And this wasn't just any man, it was *Luke*. He was a vision any woman might like to wake up to, very masculine, enticing even to a woman who was *never* enticed. Dressed in flannel and denim and a heavy coat, his hair slightly mussed as if he'd run his fingers through it several times this morning, his shoulders broad and his legs long, he was unexpectedly tempting. Even in her waking moments, Faith Martin never gave in to temptation!

Luke's weight made the mattress dip, and it was an effort for Faith to keep herself from gently sliding into him. She still remembered last night's kiss. How could she not? The position she found herself in this morning was very intimate, intriguing. Something deep inside her wanted to let loose and drift into and against the man on her bed. Faith pointedly ignored that temptation, as she ignored all others.

Luke reached out and touched her face, very gently. Faith reacted, tensing momentarily then relaxing and allowing herself to enjoy the caress.

"A deep sleeper," he said. "I'm glad that's all it was. I feel like an idiot for overreacting, but…"

"But what?"

"I thought you were sick," he said gently. "You've

been handling that stuff more than anyone. I know you've been careful. I know you claim you never get sick. Still..." He shrugged his shoulders and glanced away. "Let's just say I was worried and leave it at that."

Faith nodded. What had she been dreaming about that made her tremble still? It was more than Luke's presence here that made her quiver. Something of a dream clung to her, made her blood rush cold through her veins. She could not remember the nightmare, and in truth she didn't want to. This moment was much nicer than any dream, good or bad.

"The rescue was unnecessary, but I do thank you," she said. "It was very nice of you to be worried."

When Luke did not respond, she glanced up to see that he had his eyes locked on her in an intense and not entirely casual way. She shivered but hid the response by shifting the covers and pulling them closer.

"Who's Mark?" he asked in a lowered voice.

Wide-eyed and confused, Faith answered, "I have no idea."

"You called out his name in your sleep."

"I don't know anyone named Mark." She believed that statement, for a moment, and then a few of Jake Ingram's words penetrated the fog. *Don't you remember Mark? The two of you were so close.* "No," she said more forcefully. "I don't know anyone by that name."

Luke kept a close eye on Faith all day. He didn't understand what was happening to her, but whatever it was, he didn't like it. She looked as though she hadn't slept at all, and she'd eaten practically nothing for breakfast. He'd walked into her lab once and caught her rooting around in the trash can. She'd looked so guilty when she'd glanced up and found him there that he hadn't even bothered to ask what she was searching for.

The citizens of Rockland were unhappy about being quarantined, but they made the best of the situation by granting telephone interviews and sharing their opinions with the reporters who had been quarantined along with the citizens. Rockland Fever was big news, especially now that the public knew the virus had been manufactured in a lab. Bioterrorism had struck in the heartland; everyone was vulnerable. If it could happen here, it could happen anywhere.

All the patients improved, and there were no new cases to treat. Until the haz-mat team that had arrived with the National Guard had examined the homes of everyone in the county and declared the area free of the contaminant, no one was going anywhere.

Fine by him. There was no longer any compelling reason for Faith to stay here in Rockland. She could pack up her findings and take them to a more well equipped lab in D.C. for study, as soon as she was able. She probably couldn't wait to get out of here. Would she even give Carson County a second thought in the months to come? What about him?

Probably not.

Too bad. He really would like to take her fishing, among other things. He had a feeling—no, he *knew*— that there was more to Faith Martin than met the eye. He wanted to uncover the real person, the woman she hid beneath the lab coat. He'd never get that chance.

The day had passed too quickly, in that way hectic days can. Luke loitered outside the lab, waiting for Faith to exit. Maybe she planned to stay in there all night. He doubted it would be the first time she'd worked around the clock. Still, she was in no shape to work these kinds of hours. Especially not after a night like last night.

He was so intent on the door to the makeshift lab, he didn't see Molly coming until she stood right beside him. "Is she in there?"

Luke nodded. "Yeah."

Molly, who looked much better for her night off, leaned against the wall. "There's something fishy going on here," she observed.

Luke laughed. "You think?"

Molly waved a dismissive hand. "Don't sass me. You might be the doctor around here, but I've got a few years on you."

"Sorry, ma'am."

She sighed. "No, I'm not talking about the virus or the National Guard or the quarantine."

Luke's attention returned to the lab door. "Then what are you talking about?"

"First of all, Betsy has been flirting with Dr. White."

Betsy was the Carson County Clinic's part-time nurse who had become full-time the moment the epidemic hit. She was pretty enough, though not gorgeous, but she was very shy. Carrying on a conversation, especially with a man, made her visibly nervous. The people who knew Betsy well had learned to live with the fact that every time she opened her mouth there was a chance she'd put her foot in it. And she'd been flirting? How was that possible?

"Are you sure?"

"Positive," Molly said, not sounding particularly happy. "I'm glad she finally found a guy she likes, I really am, but Dr. White is not going to stay in Rockland. What if he breaks her heart, Luke? You know how Betsy is. She might never recover from something like that. Why couldn't she have fallen for Michael Franklin or one of the Whitlaw boys?''

''Maybe it's not that serious,'' Luke suggested.

Molly snorted. ''I hope you're right. But I swear, it looks serious enough to me.''

''What do you want me to do?''

''Talk to Dr. White,'' she ordered. ''Tell him if he trifles with Betsy he'll have to answer to you.''

Luke stared in disbelief at his nurse. ''I'm not her father, Molly. Or her big brother. What she does on her own time is none of my business. I certainly can't go around threatening the men she flirts with.''

Molly's expression was formidable. ''Well, you could have a little man-to-man talk with him.''

Luke sighed. ''I'll see what I can do.''

She lowered her voice. ''And that's not all that's fishy around here.''

Great. Had one of the lab nerds made a pass at the Bozeman nurses?

''Yesterday a man called for Dr. Martin.'' Molly moved a little bit closer. ''Said his name was Jake Ingram. Why is that name familiar?''

Faith had asked about Ingram last night. Now Luke knew why. ''He's some financial hotshot. Rich guy from Texas. Now that I think of it, didn't he have something to do with that World Bank heist a few months back? Trying to solve the crime, not planning it,'' he clarified.

''Yeah!'' Molly said in a brighter voice. ''That's where I saw his name, in the newspaper. Anyway, he

called yesterday, and I think he upset Dr. Martin. He's
called three times today."

"Three times?"

Molly nodded.

"Did Dr. Martin talk to him?"

"No. He didn't even ask to speak to her."

"What the hell did he want, then?"

Again Molly lowered her voice. "He wanted to
know if Dr. Martin was here, and if she seemed okay,
and if I had given her his cell phone number like he
asked me to. I did give her the number, of course, but
she didn't seem interested in calling him. Like I said,
I think he upset her."

"You're right, Molly. Fishy."

She snorted. "If there was no quarantine, Ingram
would be here, I'll betcha. He sounded kinda frustrated
over the phone, especially that last time. I think he's
expecting Dr. Martin to call him, she's not having anything to do with him, and he's getting antsy waiting
for the phone to ring."

"Thanks," Luke said, pushing away from the wall
and heading for the lab where Faith had worked all
day and into the night. "I'll take care of it."

"How?" she asked.

Luke mumbled as he pushed into the lab. "I have
no idea."


"You shouldn't be in here," Faith said as Luke
stormed through the door and into the makeshift lab
like a tornado. Did he always barge in wherever he
went? It certainly seemed that way. Luke Winston was
disorder among the order she loved so well. The order
she needed.

"Neither should you." He stopped a few feet from

the door, crossed his arms over his chest and glared at her. She felt that glare from the tips of her toes to the top of her head.

The contagion was safely contained, so that was not a problem. Still, no one wanted to get too close to the virus. No one but her.

"Is everything all right?" she asked, wondering why Luke had come barging in with that cheerless expression on his face. So far the antibiotic was doing its job. The only thing that could make this day any worse was the news that one of the victims of the virus had taken a turn for the worse.

"The patients are all doing well, if that's what you mean," Luke assured her. "Since they're improving, the nurses have each been able to get more rest, so they're doing well, too. The haz-mat team that's been searching for more of your greenish-yellow powder hasn't found any more, thank God. So yeah, for the most part everything is all right."

"For the most part?"

He shook his head. "You're dead on your feet, Faith. Am I going to have to drag you out of here every night?"

*Only until I leave Carson County and you behind me.* She should argue with him, tell him that she was an adult who was perfectly capable of setting her own work hours.

But she was tired. Tired and bewildered. "I've accomplished all I can today," she admitted. "I don't know why I'm so fatigued. In the past I've worked longer hours than this without any ill effects." And he was right. She was dead on her feet.

"You didn't sleep well last night," Luke said, a kind softening to his deep voice.

Remnants of a nightmare came back to her, and she shuddered as she pushed the memory deep. ''No, I guess I didn't.''

It was more than the nightmare that had bothered her throughout the day. She fingered the crumpled sheet of paper she carried in her lab coat pocket—Jake Ingram's cell phone number, retrieved from the trash can. Was there any truth at all in his fantastic story? Questions she did not want to ask filled her mind, distracted her from her work. Nothing ever distracted her, and yet here she was—Luke on one hand, a mysterious caller who claimed to be her brother on the other.

''The café delivered some food a little while ago, if you're hungry,'' Luke said.

At the suggestion, her stomach growled.

''We can eat in my office.''

It was an offer she could not refuse. As she and Luke walked down the hallway, side by side, Faith shoved her hand into her pocket and touched the wrinkled piece of paper that had been calling her since the moment she'd dug it out of the trash. She didn't know if it was yesterday's phone conversation or the nightmare, or a combination of the two, but all day her mind had been spinning.

She had never remembered anything of her life before going to live with the Martins. No warm or frightening childhood memories teased her, and no flashes of the past intruded on her day-to-day life. Her memory was excellent, and always had been, but her life before ten was nonexistent in her mind.

Until today. In fragments of memory that were clear and sharp she remembered the smell of fragrant flowers and the patter of warm rain, a smiling woman, children. There were other memories that were less pleasant, memories of being afraid. Of hiding. Of deep, salty water that threatened to drag her down.

The most vivid recollection was of a boy helping her to the surface, pulling her from that salty water. He was much stronger than any child should be, and yet if her memory was correct, he had saved her. She still couldn't see his face, not clearly, but she knew it was Mark. The brother who yesterday, and again this morning, she had insisted she did not remember.

Her neat little world had been turned upside down. She wanted to convince herself that everything Jake Ingram had said to her was a lie. She didn't know why he would tell her such an outrageous story, but it had to be a lie.

Try as she might she could not convince herself that what he'd told her was false. In fact, as the day had passed, she'd been more and more sure that he'd been telling her the truth.

All her life, Faith had realized she was different. She knew it, and so did everyone else. The people who loved her—Nash and their parents—said she wasn't odd but special. Gifted. An extraordinary woman. But that wasn't quite right, was it?

She was a freak. A genetically engineered experiment, not unlike the manufactured virus she'd been studying all day. She was a product of science, not nature. No wonder she had always felt different. She *was* different, in the most horrible way.

Her occasional glimpses of a potential normal life in her future were fantasy. There would be nothing resembling normalcy in her coming years. No husband, no children...no family at all. Who in their right mind would want to be associated with a freak?

The smell of food assaulted her as Luke opened the door to his office. The aroma almost knocked her off her feet. Her stomach churned, and she swayed on her feet.

"Whoa." Luke grabbed her arm and steadied her. "You're in worse shape than I thought." He led her to the nearest chair, the one at his desk, and continued to hold her as she sat. There before her, bigger than life, sat his telephone.

"The food's in the other room." He nodded toward the open door to the anteroom where she had slept a few days ago. Where Luke had caught her wearing nothing but a towel. "I'll make you a plate and get you something to drink, and then we'll see about—"

"Luke," she interrupted. "I need...I have to..." He stared at her, waiting. "I need to make a couple of phone calls," she said softly. "Do you mind?"

He hesitated. "Are you sure you're all right?"

She nodded, and after a moment Luke reluctantly left her alone in his office. She had a suspicion he was waiting just outside the door, and if she needed him all she had to do was call his name. Silly notion. She didn't need him or anyone else.

Her first call was to her brother, Nash. Her real brother, the one she remembered. The brother who'd come into her life when she was ten and he was twelve. She breathed a sigh of relief when he answered the phone.

"Nash?" she said, her voice much weaker than she'd intended.

"Faith!" She could hear the smile in his voice. "I'm so glad you called. I missed your phone call when you got back in the country, and then I saw you on the news, and— Everything there is all right, isn't it? I tried your cell a couple of times.''

"I don't get a signal here," she explained.

"That's what you get for working in the boonies all the time," he teased. "So, are you okay? You sound tired."

"I'm fine," she said. In truth, she wasn't fine and never would be again, but there was no time to explain her turmoil. Besides, how could she ever tell Nash the truth about herself? "I just have a minute, but I wanted to ask you a question."

"Shoot."

Faith took a deep breath. "When I first came to live with Mom and Dad and you, did I say anything that struck you as odd?"

Nash laughed lightly. "You didn't say anything at all for weeks. Mom said you'd been traumatized by your parents being killed in the car crash, so I cut you some slack."

Nash had done more than cut her some slack. He had always been there for her. Always. Their personalities were as different as night and day, and always had been. She was a scientist who appreciated order and concrete answers. He was a sculptor whose work struck her as anything but conventional. She needed control. Nash was likely to take off at a moment's notice without telling anyone where he was going or when he'd be back. They'd been just as dissimilar as children as they were as adults, and yet they had been close.

"So, I was quiet," she said.

"More than quiet, you were very withdrawn. Almost catatonic." Nash's voice had become more somber. "I remember Mom being worried that you'd never snap out of it, but you did. Eventually. What's this about?''

She couldn't tell him the truth, not now, not over the phone. Maybe not ever. ''Just wondering,'' she said absently. ''I can't wait to see you,'' she added quickly, before Nash had a chance to ask again why she had found a sudden interest in her past. ''As soon as the quarantine is lifted, I'll fly down and pay you a visit.''

''Great!'' he said. ''I've missed you.''

''I've missed you, too.'' It was the truth. Diverse as their personalities were, she and Nash had bonded at an early age. They had been as close as any real brother and sister could possibly be. ''See you soon,'' she said. ''Love you.''

''Love you, too.''

Faith severed the connection before she could say more. And then, before she could lose her courage, she took the piece of paper from her lab coat pocket, laid it on the desk and flattened it with the palm of her hand, and dialed another number.

A man's gruff voice answered, ''Ingram.''

She took a deep breath, ''Mr. Ingram, this is Faith Martin.''

''Faith. I'm so glad you called.''

''I've been thinking about what you told me yesterday,'' she said. Her heart pounded, her blood pressure rose markedly.

''Did our conversation spark some lost memories?'' he asked.

''Yes.''

His sigh was one of relief, or so it seemed. ''I tried to get clearance to fly into Carson County, but—''

''No!'' Faith interrupted. ''Don't come here.'' It

was more than worry for another's health that made her order him to stay away. She wanted these last few days of normalcy, before her life changed forever. She wanted, for a few more days, to be Faith Martin, woman, before Jake Ingram turned her life inside out and she became Faith the lab experiment. "It's not safe," she added, so he would not know where her mind had taken her.

"I can get clearance. It'll just take a few more hours to cut through the red tape."

"No," Faith said again, more forcefully this time. "Mr. Ingram—"

"Jake," he said. "After all, I am your brother."

She knew that was true, knew it without a doubt. But she didn't *feel* it. Would she ever?

"Jake," she began again, "I have a few questions."

"Ask me anything."

# Eight

Faith had made her phone calls, and afterward she'd eaten a little bit. Luke couldn't help but wonder if one of those calls had been to Jake Ingram. She hadn't said, and he didn't ask.

Again tonight he drove her to the motel. She'd protested once that she needed to work a few hours more, but she had not protested long or hard. That was good, because he was prepared to toss her over his shoulder and carry her out of the clinic, if need be. When had this desire to take care of her grown so strong?

Abby had a place of her own; he was her father, she was his little girl. Caring for her was a responsibility and a joy that went so deep it could never be shaken. He took care of patients every day, and he tried to keep an eye on Molly and Nelda, women who were so busy watching over everyone else they occasionally forgot about themselves.

Taking care of Faith felt different, somehow. Special. And scary.

Tonight he didn't watch from the driver's seat while she walked to the door. He turned off the engine and exited the SUV as Faith stepped down and into the parking lot. She glanced over her shoulder quickly, obviously surprised that he was leaving the vehicle, but she didn't order him to get back behind the wheel and go home.

Faith unlocked the door to her room, and Luke followed her inside. It was too cold to stand on her doorstep like a couple of sixteen-year-olds, braving the icy wind while he tried to decide whether or not he was going to kiss her again.

She shed her coat and dropped it over a chair, her back to him. There was nothing sexy about the way Faith dressed. Her tan sweater was too big, her brown trousers were plain. But she could wear a burlap sack and look good in it. The sensuality wasn't in the clothes; it was in the way she wore them, in the way she moved.

Luke didn't remove his coat; he didn't yet know if he'd be staying more than a few minutes.

"I'm worried about you," he said in a low voice. "You've been working too hard, and you're obviously not sleeping well."

"I'll be fine," she said without enthusiasm.

"Will you?"

Faith turned to face him, tilted her chin up so she could look him in the eye. "You're not here in my room because you're worried about me."

"Not entirely," he said honestly.

Faith began to respond and then hesitated. The uncertainty she felt was evident, not only on her face but in the way she held her body. Luke wanted to reach out and touch her, tell her she could say anything, do anything. He wanted her to be free with him, but already he knew Faith well enough to know she was never completely free.

"Last night you kissed me," she said. "That was entirely inappropriate behavior, given the circumstances, but I can't say I was entirely opposed to your overture."

"Glad to hear it."

Faith took a deep breath and squared her shoulders. "There's been something awkward between us from my first day here."

Once she found her courage, she got right to the point. He should have known Faith would not be anything other than straightforward. "I guess there has been."

"I believe I can explain what's been happening," she said.

He didn't want her to explain anything. He wanted a signal from her, no matter how small, that she wanted him to kiss her again. "Go ahead."

She swallowed hard, and her fingers trembled. Good, at least she was nervous about delivering her explanation.

"Before I was called here to Carson County, I had been contemplating whether or not I will ever have children."

Not what he'd been expecting, as explanations went. "The old biological clock," he said irreverently.

"Yes," she whispered. "You see, no matter how advanced we become as a society, deep inside we continue to possess the same animal instincts that drove our ancestors to survive. It's certainly no longer imperative to the survival of our species that we pair-bond and procreate, but the desire to do so survives."

After hearing her rationalization, Luke had a feeling he wouldn't be here long enough to take off his coat. "So, you're saying this *awkwardness* between us is nothing more than the result of the untimely ticking of your biological clock."

"Yes." Calm and very professional, Faith continued. "In my most primal self, the part of me that can't be educated into oblivion, I see in you a potential mate. You're intelligent, healthy…''

''Be still my heart,'' Luke muttered.

''You're handsome, too,'' she added, almost grudgingly. ''But I'm not sure that's the most important aspect. My primal response is disturbing, I'll admit to that. The point is—''

''Dammit, I knew there was going to be a point,'' Luke mumbled.

Faith ignored his interruption. ''There's a perfectly reasonable explanation for these awkward moments, and as intelligent human beings we can set our minds to rise above our instincts.''

She stared up at him, those wide blue eyes tired but discerning, naive but filled with passion she apparently did not understand.

''My turn?'' he asked.

''If you have anything pertinent to say, I believe this is the time to do so.''

He took a single small step to bring himself closer to Faith, so close he could feel her body heat. ''First of all, stop calling what's going on with us *awkwardness*. It's sexual attraction.''

''Call it whatever you like,'' Faith said softly. In spite of her attempt to be intellectually detached, she blushed.

''And if it's so easy to explain away, then why me? There are three doctors, all intelligent and healthy, on your team. Wouldn't one of the geeks satisfy your primal instincts?''

''Apparently not,'' she muttered.

He reached out and brushed a misbehaving strand of dark hair away from a pale cheek. ''You do respond to me, Faith. I see it in you. You can try to explain it away all night, if you want, but that doesn't change anything. That aside, I respond to you, too. Surely you know that by now. What's *my* excuse, Doctor?''

"I don't know," she admitted. "You could be experiencing a chemical reaction in response to my primitive drive to reproduce, I suppose.''

"Chemistry, biology, anthropology." He leaned down so that his nose almost touched hers. "What about love, Dr. Martin?''

She swallowed hard. "I'm talking about science. Fact. Not…fantasy.''

"Do you think love is nothing more than a fantasy?'' he whispered.

"Yes.''

Frustrated as he was by Faith's maddening rationale, he couldn't make himself walk away. He leaned in, tilted his head and laid his lips over hers. It was impossible to be this close to the woman and not kiss her. For all her arguments, for all her damned sensibility, she kissed him back this time.

In his months of grief, he had forgotten all about the power of a kiss. There was more to a man and woman coming together, much more, but a kiss had an energy all its own. It was a potential beginning. It was a test. Did her mouth fit his just so? Yes. Did he have the brainpower to wonder what would happen next while they kissed? No. There was only mouth to mouth and a world of possibilities. He tasted Faith. He felt her to his bones.

"So," Luke said when he very reluctantly took his mouth from Faith's. "You think the only reason the world rocks when I kiss you is because you want a baby and I'm *here*.''

She nodded. Once.

He didn't believe it. Couldn't. "What if I told you that I can't give you a child." He traced a finger along Faith's jawline and she shuddered. "I have a low sperm count. Very low. The lowest. I'm shooting blanks. As a caveman who's responsible for the survival of mankind, I'm a dismal failure."

"Really?"

He kissed her again, deeper this time. Longer and harder. She opened up to him like a flower in the rain, soft and yielding. He didn't stop with a kiss, not this time. He touched her, holding her head so she couldn't move away, wrapping one arm around her and pulling her close, so she could feel for herself just how primitive this moment was.

Eyes closed, lips parted, tongue dancing, Faith answered his kiss as if she was starving for him. Just him. No one but him.

He took his mouth from hers and whispered, "Still want me?"

"Yes," she said breathlessly.

"Even if I can't give you everything you want?"

"Yes." Her voice became husky, rasping over him as she grasped his coat and held on tight.

"Then I'd say your theory is a load of horse hockey."

She released her hold on him and backed away, surprise in her eyes, a tremble in her lips.

"It's okay." He touched Faith's face gently, unsure as to how she would react to something so simple after the kiss that had made his knees week. "You don't have to be able to rationalize every moment of your life. Life is not an experiment. We don't live in a lab."

She drew away from him as if he'd slapped her, but

the surprise on her face and the tension in her stance faded quickly.

"You have Abby," she said hoarsely. "How is that possible if you're…" She couldn't bring herself to say it.

"I said *what if*," he countered. "As far as I know, my sperm count is fine. But when I kissed you it didn't matter." *Explain that, Doctor.*

Faith brushed the hair away from her face. Ah, good. For once, she didn't have a quick, neat answer.

"I really need to get to bed," she said.

"I agree."

She glanced at him sharply. A moment ago she'd been on the verge of losing control. That control had come back with a vengeance. "Alone."

"Unfortunately, I agree with that, too." He turned toward the door, ready to face the cold wind once again. He knew it was for the best. Faith was not ready for what he wanted. She wasn't ready to give anything of herself, not to him or anyone else, he imagined. She was so safe and comfortable in her small, controlled, neat little world she didn't know what to do when it was rocked.

He knew this was best, but he didn't want to leave. Not yet. His back to Faith, his hand on the doorknob, he said, "I didn't get to finish telling you what I think."

She didn't urge him to continue, but she didn't tell him to get lost, either. Luke glanced over his shoulder. "I like you. You're smart, you know what you want and go for it, and you care for the people around you more than you let on. On top of that, you're the most beautiful, most exciting woman I've ever known."

"I'm not—"

"Let me finish."

She closed her mouth and clasped her hands.

"You're right about one thing. What I want from you, what I'm experiencing right now, is primitive. I can feel you inside me, Faith. I crave you in a way I didn't think was possible. My emotions and desires are not logical, and I don't expect them to be. I can't explain them away, and I'm not even going to try."

Faith looked tired, scared…vulnerable. He wanted to wrap his arms around her again, but now was not the time. "And, Faith, I do believe in love."

She should let Luke walk out the door. Tomorrow she would be stronger, not so tired, not shaken to her core by the news that she had been conceived in a scientific experiment and was a perversion of nature.

Luke didn't think she was a perversion. He liked her. He even thought she was beautiful.

Now that he'd had his say, he was going to leave. It took all the bravery she possessed to cross the room, to lay her hand over Luke's. To stop him from walking away.

"Don't go," she whispered quickly, before she lost her courage.

Luke didn't make her ask twice, and he didn't ask her why she'd changed her mind. He just turned and took her in his arms and kissed her again.

She'd been trying so hard to reason this longing away, but Luke was right when he said everything in life didn't need to be analyzed. It was all right to feel, to experience, to take. She had never been impulsive, but she wanted to be impulsive tonight.

Her life was about to change. For tonight, just for tonight, she didn't want to be an experiment or an oddity. She wanted to be a woman. Luke made her feel like she was a woman. Nothing more, nothing less.

"Do you have a condom?" she asked breathlessly. She might long for a child of her own, in the recesses of her mind, but she didn't want a baby as a result of a one-night stand. That was all this could be. One night. She didn't want to drag Luke into her life against his will, just because they had made a child together.

"Yes."

Faith didn't ask how or why Luke had come here prepared. At the moment, she didn't care. She pushed his coat off and let it fall to the floor. He didn't dress like any doctor she had ever known. He wore red-and-blue flannel, well-worn denim and sturdy boots.

She loved his heat and the strength in his hard body, the warmth and tenderness of his kiss. Yes, when he touched her, the response of her body was deep and undeniably primitive, but she stopped trying to work her mind around all the whys. Why do I feel this way? Why him? Why now?

For the first time in her life, she shut down the questions and the rationalizations and allowed herself to feel and respond without analyzing every shudder, every leap of her heart.

They danced toward the bed slowly, kissing and touching as they stepped across the floor. Luke slipped his hand beneath her sweater and touched her side. His hand was warm and large, the contact electric. She unbuttoned his flannel shirt, anxious to touch his flesh with her hands, just as he touched hers.

When they arrived at the bed, they sat. Luke reached up and around to release her hair from its ponytail, and then he ran his fingers through the strands and kissed her so deep, her body screamed for more.

Faith's fingers trembled as she finished unbuttoning Luke's shirt. Was she really doing this? Not only inviting this man to stay the night, but undressing him because she couldn't wait any longer to touch him.

Luke took his mouth from hers and grabbed the tail end of her sweater. He lifted it slowly, then whisked it over her head.

Faith wasn't wearing a bra; she rarely did. There simply was no need. For a moment she felt incredibly awkward and exposed. She lifted her arms and covered her breasts, glanced toward the light on the bedside table. "Maybe I should turn this off."

"No," Luke said softly. He took her wrists in his hands and very gently pulled her arms away from her body, so she sat before him half bare. The way he looked at her, hungry and warm, the way a man looks at a woman he desires…that wasn't awkward, not at all. "I want to see you, Faith. You're so beautiful."

He touched her, cupping her breast and brushing his thumb across the nipple as he leaned in and kissed her again. Her nipples peaked, and at her core she fluttered. Luke kissed her deep, while his fingers explored and teased and aroused. He had a magic touch, gentle and sensual. Patient and loving.

No man had ever touched her quite this way; at the very least, her body had certainly never reacted in this way. Every nerve responded to Luke's hands and his mouth, until Faith was able to think of nothing else but the sensations that floated and rippled through her body.

And with each moment that passed, she wanted him

more. Whether the craving was unexplained passion or a return to basic instinct, she didn't know or care. She only knew that her body and his were meant to be together, that before this night was finished he would be inside her. The very thought made her clench, grow damp and ready.

With a touch of impatience, she pushed his unbuttoned shirt off his shoulders. Luke had well-defined muscles in his arms and across his chest, and she found them all fascinating. Her fingers explored those muscles, trembling just slightly. He was the beautiful one; she was glad he had insisted on leaving the light on.

She fell back on the bed, and he came with her, leaning over her as the kiss continued. Her legs spread slightly; he fit himself between them, opening her wider, and she felt his contained erection press against her.

He took his mouth from hers and moved lower, to catch and suckle a sensitive nipple. Faith arched up and into him, instinct again taking over as her hips rocked against his. Her fingers threaded through his hair and she hung on as he aroused her to a point where she could no longer think rationally. There was only sensation. Only Luke. Only her body and his.

Luke was a patient and unhurried lover. Time stopped. The room, the world, did not extend beyond this bed. Her flesh had never been so sensitive, but as Luke caressed and kissed her, the sensitivity grew. He seemed determined to taste every inch of her. Her neck, her breasts, her soft belly. When he came back to her mouth, his hands stroked and fluttered.

His body was so much harder than hers, his chest dusted with dark hair, the muscles there solid and warm. She tasted those muscles, laid her tongue against his small flat nipples, sucked at the most tender part of his throat until she made him moan.

She made Luke moan, and knowing he wanted her so much only made her need him more.

He slipped her trousers and underwear down and off, leaving her completely bare. His fingers, warm and strong, climbed her thigh to touch her intimately. She rocked against him, experienced a tightening ribbon of pleasure as he caressed her.

In spite of her initial reservations, she knew in her heart this moment was right. It was much too late for second thoughts, as if her body would allow such a diversion. Luke was special to her, in so many ways, and that made tonight special. Inevitable and precious.

And potent. Faith couldn't wait any longer. She reached down to unsnap and unzip Luke's jeans. He was so close. She wanted to reach out and touch him, to lay her hand over his length and gently stroke, but she didn't dare. Instead she traced her fingers along his waist, her fingertips barely dipping beneath the denim. He moaned low in his throat and rose up to kiss her. Her lips parted wide, his tongue speared into her mouth.

While her mouth devoured his, her hips lifted of their own accord to bring his erection closer to her core. Damp and aching, she needed him there. Now. She whispered his name when he took his mouth from hers.

He snagged a condom from his back pocket before shedding his jeans and shorts and tossing them aside, along with the boots that thudded noisily against the floor. With trembling fingers, he ripped the foil package open and sheathed himself.

And then he sheathed himself in her.

The joining of their bodies was the end, for a moment, the goal she had been spiraling toward, the answer to a longing so intense she had begun to believe that she could not live without it.

And then Luke began to move, to make love to her with the gentle sway of his hips. She stretched to accept him, as he buried himself inside her. The joining made her complete, satisfied her, but as he moved within her she found a new beginning.

The pleasure of completion swirled just out of reach as Luke moved tenderly within her. Each long stroke took him deeper. Faith wrapped her arms and her legs around him and swayed up and into his slow thrusts. They found a perfect rhythm, their own divine dance.

For all her perfectly logical arguments, Faith knew, deep down, that there was a purely emotional reason she wanted Luke and no one else. She opened her eyes and watched his face as he loved her. He was so beautiful. So good and wise and noble.

If she believed in love, she might think she'd fallen for Luke the first time she'd laid eyes on him. Love at first sight was a ridiculous concept, and yet how else could she account for the way she felt? And she did *feel*. Illogically and with a much too heavy dose of a purely feminine vulnerability, she experienced a rush of emotion she could not explain away.

Luke plunged deep and hard, and she could not think of anything else but the way he filled her. She wanted this to last all night, but all too soon they danced faster, driven by need and passion. Faith came with a hoarse cry, her body wrapped around Luke's.

Buried deep inside her, he found his release moments after she did as her inner muscles caressed and milked him.

Entwined and spent, they collapsed. Faith raked her hand down Luke's side; she had the energy for nothing more demanding. He kissed her, a gentle kiss very different from the arousing caresses they'd exchanged moments earlier.

She held on tight, as her breath fought to return. Her body continued to tremble gently, and if she cared to monitor her heart rate and blood pressure at the moment, she would find them most definitely altered.

Had she almost sent Luke away tonight? How foolish it would have been to turn her back on him, to deny what she felt for this man.

"It's lucky that you had a condom with you," Faith said when she was able to speak.

"Lucky?" Luke raised up and smiled down at her. "Honey, a man makes his own luck."

She hadn't been able to let him go earlier, but she should send him away now. *Thank you very much. That was pleasant. I'll see you tomorrow.* She held on tight. "You knew," she said softly. "You knew we would be together tonight."

He shook his head. "I hoped. There's a difference."

Hope. Earlier today she'd had none. Right now… She pushed aside all her doubts and fears of the uncertain future. She would not worry about what was to come, not tonight. She would not think about Jake Ingram and his fantastic story, the siblings she was beginning to remember, the questions about her past. Not tonight. Luke was here. He thought she was beautiful. With a glance, he made her quiver.

"Does it bother you?" he asked, his smile fading.

"That I was prepared for what happened here tonight?"

"No," she said honestly. "I'm glad. I didn't even think of…" Heavens, was she blushing? It made little difference. Her entire body was flushed, pink and warm and well loved. "I guess I didn't think at all. I'm glad one of us did."

"What am I, Faith?" Luke's smile drifted back. "An eternal optimist or a scheming lecher?"

"Well…"

"Before you answer, there's something you should see." He rolled away, reached for his jeans and delved into the pockets. When he moved his body away from hers, Faith was acutely aware of her nakedness. She grabbed the bedcover and quickly pulled it around her so that she was at least partially covered.

Luke was busy for a moment. All in all, he came up with eight condoms from various pockets.

Faith smiled as he tossed the condoms onto the bedside table. But it wasn't the shiny foil packages she thought of when she considered his question, it was the expression on his face when he'd turned to her and said, "I do believe in love."

She snaked her arm around Luke's neck and pulled him close. Eyes closed, mouth hungry, she kissed him the way he had kissed her: with everything she had to give. He answered in kind, as she had known he would.

No, she was not ready to send him on his way with a thank-you and a friendly handshake. She wanted more. She wanted him here all night long.

When she took her mouth from his, she said, "Eternal optimist. Most definitely an eternal optimist."

# Nine

One in the morning had come and gone much too quickly, and still he couldn't sleep. Luke drew a sleeping Faith closer against him. She sighed and nuzzled, and then became still. For someone who had tried very hard to explain away her feelings in an unemotional, logical manner, she was a surprisingly spirited lover.

He hadn't told Faith that she was the first woman he'd been with since his wife's sudden death. It was an uncomfortable confession, and besides, there had been no time. One minute he'd been leaving, the next she'd been drawing him to the bed and he hadn't been able to think of anything or anyone else.

Logically, he knew Faith would never be satisfied to live in a town like Rockland, not even for a few months. She'd be gone too soon, before they had a chance to discover if they had anything besides the passion she tried to reason away.

Without the interference of that annoying logic, he wanted more. Fishing, dancing, days without the stress of the epidemic pulling them in several different directions. Maybe they didn't have anything but this— sexual attraction, mutual need. No matter. They'd never have a chance to find out if there was more.

He lay there for a while holding Faith, listening to her breathe. The touch of her flesh along his was like a drug; he didn't want this night to end. He should go home. Nelda and Abby were long asleep, but in the morning they'd expect him to be there. Still he didn't want to go. Not yet. He dozed but not deeply.

Faith hadn't been sleeping long when she began to move restlessly, bringing Luke fully awake again. She didn't roll away from him, but held on tight. Her breathing changed, became shallow and uneven, and she began to mumble nonsense in her sleep.

Now and then he made out a single word among the nonsense. *No. Breathe. Mark.*

Ah. Another Mark dream. He took some small pleasure from the obvious fact that the dream was not pleasant.

Should he wake Faith and bring an end to her nightmare? She'd been sleeping so well until just a few moments ago. And she needed her sleep. Before he could make a move, the decision was taken from him when she woke with a start.

For a moment she appeared to be truly afraid and a little surprised, but the fear faded quickly and was replaced by contentment. The Faith he now held was a heavy-lidded and assured woman who looked as if she was never afraid. Of anything.

"You're still here," she said in a husky voice.

"Yeah."

She reached out and touched him, her fingers fluttering down his chest. "Good." Her eyes were hooded, sleepily sexy, curious. Dark hair that had been through his fingers many times tonight tumbled and tangled around her body. She turned her head and a few twisted strands fell over her cheek as she continued to touch him.

The room's only light came through the open bathroom door, but it was enough. In fact, the light was perfect. No bright glare dimmed the sight of Faith as she watched the gentle motion of her pale fingers on his chest, then lifted his hand and placed it where she wanted it, on her breast. She closed her eyes, tossing her head back and sighing deeply as he caressed her. ''When you touch me there I feel you all through my body,'' she whispered.

Prim Dr. Martin was, at the moment, his wild Faith.

He kissed her, and she met him with ardor, her mouth taking as well as giving, demanding more. Her tongue danced with his. Her hands were never still, her body quivered and grew warmer.

''Do you want me again?'' she whispered, tossing back the sheet to bare them both. Her body lying beside his was soft and pale, feminine and deceptively delicate. Faith might look delicate, but she was stronger than she appeared to be.

She touched him boldly, without a moment's hesitation, wrapping her fingers around his length and stroking once. He was already hard, had been since the moment she'd laid her hand on his chest.

''You know I want you,'' he answered.

She smiled and cocked her head to one side. ''Prove it,'' she whispered. ''Make me shudder, Luke. Make me scream.'' She latched her mouth to his, parted her lips and kissed him deeply.

He rolled her onto her back and parted her thighs with his knees. She laughed lightly. ''Not so fast, lover. We have all night.'' With a gentle shove, she rolled Luke onto *his* back.

*Lover?* He dismissed the strange endearment when Faith leaned over him and gave him a sexy smile.

''I've never done anything like this before, you know.''

He suspected she was telling the truth.

"I've always been afraid to tell the few men who have been in my life what I want, what I feel." She leaned forward and nuzzled against him, kissed his neck while she stroked his length with a maddeningly light touch. Her mouth came to rest against his ear. "I'm not afraid right now," she whispered.

No, she was certainly *not* afraid.

"You make me quiver," she said softly. She tilted her head and teased his neck for a moment, sucking lightly, trailing the tip of her tongue there. "No man has ever made me burn, not like this. I throb, Luke. I ache and yearn, and something savage grows until I can no longer contain it. I want you inside me again, and again. I will never get enough of you."

There had been a touch of nervousness in the air when they'd come together the first time. Was it always that way with a first time? He had forgotten, it had been so long. Still, a little wariness in this particular situation seemed right. Natural.

Faith knew no nervousness this time, she had no reservations of any kind. She touched him as she pleased, guided his hands with abandon when she wanted to be touched. The sight of her delicate hand shifting his to lay it over her breast again erased any reservations he might have. The way she moaned when he tweaked the nipple gently washed away any sense of uneasiness he might have experienced when she awoke seeming slightly...different.

And that was just the beginning.

Faith tasted and explored and moaned. It was as if she'd never seen or touched a man's body before, and she wanted to acquaint herself with every curve. Not only that, she tested him, searching for and finding the places on his body where her hands and mouth could drive him wild. No, beyond wild.

When she had roused him to the point where he could no longer think, she once again grasped and guided his hand. This time she laid his fingers on the soft flesh of her inner thigh, urged those fingers higher, then tossed her head back and sighed when he caressed her. Her hair fell over her shoulders and down her back, swaying gently in time with his caress.

Almost abruptly she moved away, tossing herself onto her back and moaning gently. She stretched across the bed, and as Luke rolled atop her she put her arms around him and drew him close, guided his body to hers as she whispered, "I suspect these bodies were made for nights like this. My body for yours. Yours for mine." She licked her lips and told him, in a most direct and inelegant way, exactly what she wanted him to do.

He almost forgot to grab a condom from the bedside table, but he had not completely lost his mind. Not yet. They made love harder this time, faster. Faith didn't just moan when she found release, she screamed. Her nails raked down his back, her body convulsed under and around his, and while their bodies shuddered and then toppled, she whispered his name. Three times.

Faith stretched like a cat, smiled and opened her eyes slowly. She caressed his face with tender fingers and feathered quick kisses over his mouth. Her tongue flicked in and out, as if she were hungry for his taste.

So it was certainly surprising when she said, "You have to go now."

"What?"

"I have work to do." She kissed him gently, then not so gently.

"Work? No," he protested. "You need to sleep."

Faith smiled and moved against him, her body undulating slowly. "I won't get any sleep if you stay."

She had a point.

She didn't rush him from the room, not exactly, but she did very gently assist him in getting ready to go. His clothes were handed to him, while Faith did not bother to dress or even to wrap herself in the sheet. He had sensed a little bit of modesty in her earlier, when he'd first removed her sweater, but now she had none. None at all.

At the door a naked Faith handed him his coat. As he slipped it on, she kissed him. No hands, no cuddling, just mouth to mouth in a way that was surprisingly erotic. While the kiss continued, she reached around him and opened the door. At two in the morning there was no one about, which was a good thing since she held the door wide-open and continued to kiss him, mouth open and tongue teasing. He was cold. She had to be freezing with that wind buffeting her bare skin.

She took her mouth from his, muttered good-night and slammed the door in his face.

Luke stared at Faith's motel room door, more than a little stunned.

And feeling as if he'd made love to two very different women tonight.

Faith woke alone. Naked, cold and alone. She glanced around to see if perhaps Luke was in the bathroom, but no one stirred. He was gone.

She should be disappointed that he'd slip out in the

night without saying a word, but he surely had his reasons. It was considerate of him not to wake her, right? So why did it hurt? Her heart grew heavy, and she blinked back a hint of moisture that stung her eyes. Her evening with Luke had been a one-night stand, not a romantic interlude! She had no right to expect anything of him.

Sun broke through the tiny part in the drapes. Sun! Faith sat up straight, then glanced at the bedside clock. Eight o'clock! She never slept so late. Why had Luke allowed her to sleep so long?

As she swung her legs over the side of the bed she glimpsed the condoms that were left from last night. They were scattered across the table, where Luke had tossed them so casually. Seven? Hadn't there been eight? He'd only used the one, but that had been before he'd emptied his pockets. And then he'd disappeared while she slept.

Faith shook her head and pushed her hair away from her face. Maybe she'd miscounted. She had been thinking less than clearly at the time.

Even if Luke had walked out without kissing her goodbye, even if taking him as a lover was a bad idea, she could not be sorry. She'd never known a night like that, and never would again. For some reason Luke found her beautiful. He saw her as a woman, nothing else. Nothing more. She'd needed that last night. For that gift, she would always be grateful.

She showered and dressed, prepared to walk to the clinic if necessary. But when she stepped outside her motel room, she discovered an army private waiting to escort her. The young soldier said Dr. Winston had requested that he be there to transport her when she was ready to go to the clinic, and to keep anyone else from disturbing her.

So, Luke was more considerate than she'd thought, when she'd first awakened and found him gone. That took some of the sting out of waking up and finding his side of the bed cold.

She was still tired. Faith yawned as the soldier drove her to the clinic in an old green jeep. She didn't want to think about last night and this morning's rude awakening, so she watched the town of Rockland go past her window. No wonder Luke loved it so! There was so much beauty here, and more than that, there was kindness. In the people, in the very atmosphere. It was a good place to live, to raise a child.

Her driver had been silent most of the way, but when they turned into the clinic parking lot, he asked quickly, "Is everything going to be all right, ma'am?"

"What?" His questions jerked her away from her newfound appreciation of Rockland.

"With the virus, ma'am," the young man clarified as he pulled into a parking space. He was armed, dressed as a soldier and barely old enough to shave.

She glanced at the name on his uniform. Mimms. "It could have been much worse," she said honestly. "As I'm sure you've heard, this particular virus doesn't spread from person to person, and it does respond well to a particular antibiotic. It's also fortunate that the afflicted area thus far has been isolated and small."

"Yeah," Private Mimms said, turning to her as he shut off the engine. "I just kinda wondered why, you know? Why here? If someone wanted to attack the country this way, why not a larger city?"

She'd asked herself the same question, and had only

come up with one sensible answer. "I believe this must've been a test of some kind."

The young man blanched. "That crossed my mind."

"Since we've been able to treat the virus effectively, I would consider this test a failure," she said, trying to assure him that all would be well.

Private Mimms was not easily comforted. "Since this test failed, what happens next?"

*They will try again. They will launch a new attack with something deadlier, quicker, tougher to treat.* "One crisis at a time, soldier," Faith said in a light-hearted voice.

Mimms escorted her to the clinic, past the reporters who shouted questions and to the second floor. When the elevator doors opened, Luke was waiting. Maybe he'd been standing there awhile, then again maybe he'd been watching the parking lot for her arrival. Whatever the procedure had been, he was definitely waiting for her.

"Good morning," Faith said as she stepped off the elevator. It was difficult to treat Luke as she had since coming here, to speak and behave normally when she still remembered what had happened last night. She was thirty-three years old, he was older. Neither of them was romantically attached. She should not be at all embarrassed.

But there was no denying who she was. Last night had been an unusual event for her, one she did not regret.

Luke didn't look as if he'd passed a restful night himself. As usual, he was coiled pretty tight. She half expected a smile but didn't get one.

They had never really spoken about Luke's late

wife. Faith's heart did a sickening flip-flop. Did he still love the woman he had lost? Had he been thinking of her last night?

"You slept late," he said, almost accusatory.

"Yes, I did."

Private Mimms stepped away, leaving Faith and Luke alone. They wouldn't be alone long. The second floor was a busy place, and the lab called her, as it always did. Right now, the safety of the lab seemed very comforting. She couldn't get there fast enough.

"Are you all right?" Luke asked in a lowered voice.

Faith nodded. She wanted to ask him why he'd left without saying goodbye, but she didn't really want to hear his answer. Whatever his reason for sneaking out, it couldn't be good. Maybe he had been thinking of his late wife and suffered from guilt. Maybe he was sorry. Maybe she had disappointed him.

Maybe he knew the truth about her.

"I have to get to work," she said, turning away abruptly.

Luke said nothing as Faith walked quickly to the lab. Where she belonged.

He had to get out of the clinic for a little while. The patients were all stable, there were no new cases of the virus, and Faith continued to act as if he didn't exist. It had been a long damn day.

Luke walked toward home. He needed to see Abby, even if only for a few minutes. Since this epidemic had begun, he hadn't had time for his daughter. There was nothing to be done for what had already happened, but now... Maybe it was Faith's talk about having a child of her own that made him realize, in spite of everything that had happened, how lucky he was to have Abby in his life.

Lucky, yes, but was it enough? Or should he be foolish enough to try his hand at love again?

The last thing he needed or wanted was a woman who made him question everything he'd done. Faith did just that. She confused the hell out of him! One minute he wanted to shelter her, the next he wanted her in a much more earthy way.

And last night... This morning...

"Hey, Dr. Winston," an overly friendly voice called.

Luke sighed, grumbled and turned. The little red-headed reporter from Bozeman ran toward him.

"I don't have anything to say."

"Come on," she said, her smile widening as she pulled her coat close and quickened her pace. "One teeny quote. This story is getting tedious and, in case you've forgotten, I'm stuck here like everyone else."

Mitzi had a tenacious quality about her. He suspected she didn't give up easily. "Sorry. I don't have anything newsworthy for you. If you want to know how long the quarantine will last, talk to the major who arrived with the National Guard. If you want details about the virus itself, talk to Dr. Martin." With that, he turned his back on her.

Mitzi didn't leave but fell into step beside him. "What about that Dr. Martin?" she asked conversationally.

"What about her?"

"You two certainly have been spending a lot of time together," Mitzi said suggestively.

Luke glared down at the top of her red head. The last thing he or Faith needed was for their involvement, no matter how brief or unwise, to hit the news-papers. "I suppose. This virus has affected my clinic and my patients, and she's in charge of the lab. The fact that we've spent time together is hardly news-worthy."

"Don't worry. This is all off the record."

Off the record. Why didn't he trust her? Why did he feel like someone had crosshairs squarely on the back of his neck?

"Dr. Martin is kind of attractive, I guess," Mitzi continued, undaunted by Luke's silence. "Well, she would be if she'd put on some makeup and maybe invest in some clothes that weren't so baggy you can hardly tell she's a woman."

Luke bit back his defense of Faith. He had a feeling that was just what Mitzi was fishing for.

"She's smart, too," the reporter continued. "Very smart. Do guys find that kind of intelligence a turn-on? Or does it just make you worry that maybe she's smarter than you are?"

"Given the situation," Luke said tersely, "I'm ex-tremely grateful for Dr. Martin's intelligence."

Mitzi grinned. "I can understand that."

Home was close, straight ahead. "Goodbye," Luke said. "Sorry I couldn't be of any help."

She did not turn back. "Why don't you introduce me to the family? You have a little girl, right? Abby."

A chill danced up his spine. How did she know about Abby?

"Don't look so worried," she added. "I'm not stalking you. This is a small town, and I've been here more than a week. Almost two! People talk. I listen. That's my job, Dr. Winston."

He only had a few minutes to spend with Abby

before he'd need to return to the clinic, and he didn't want to share his daughter. Not tonight. "Maybe another time."

"Sure." Mitzi took a step back. Judging by the grin, her feelings had not been hurt by his refusal. "See you around."

A few more dull days like today, and the crisis would be over. The quarantine would be lifted, his clinic would return to normal, the reporters would leave town…and so would Faith.

In so many ways, he prayed for the day when his life returned to normal. But he would miss Faith when she was gone. More than he wanted to admit, more than was wise. She'd been in his life a matter of days, so why was he so certain that life would be changed forever if she wasn't in it?

Sex, he decided with a frown. That was what muddled his mind and made him think he might actually need Faith in some bone-deep way. What they had was just sex, and he was too old and too smart to be confusing physical intimacy with the real thing.

When he opened the front door, Abby, who was sitting on the floor surrounded by her favorite dolls, smiled widely and clambered to her feet. She walked toward him, that smile never fading, her chubby little legs carrying her as fast as they could.

Luke forgot everything else as he dipped down to greet his daughter with open arms.

# Ten

Faith closed the door to Luke's office and sat at his desk, impatiently dialing Jake Ingram's cell phone number. Molly insisted that he'd sounded desperate to talk to her, when he'd called an hour ago. Faith had just now been able to bring herself to leave the lab and the virus.

Jake answered on the first ring.

"This is Faith Martin," she said, immediately realizing that the addition of her last name was unnecessary. Jake Ingram was, after all, her brother. She could no longer deny that as fact. The memories were coming to her too clearly now. They came broken and startling and unwanted, but they did come. "Faith," she said in a lowered voice.

"How are you?" Jake asked, sounding as if he were truly concerned. "Has there been any trouble? Anything...unusual?"

*Dreams. Shocking memories. A new lover.* "No," she said. "Everything's fine. Is that why you called?" She had dragged herself out of the lab simply because Jake wanted to know if she was all right? She didn't know whether to be annoyed or touched.

"No," he answered in a lowered voice. "I know a lot has been happening to you lately, and it's bound to be difficult to take it all in. Trust me, I understand."

She couldn't deny that there was compassion in

Jake's voice. And she did believe that he understood, in a way no one else could. He had learned the same truths about himself, not so long ago. "Thank you, but you really don't have to continue to monitor my daily activities by phone."

"I know," Jake said. "I do worry, but I trust that you'll take the proper precautions until we can get you to a safe place. That's not why I called."

An unexpected chill washed through Faith's body, her physical reaction to her brother's words much stronger than she'd anticipated. She didn't need any more surprises in her life, not now! "Why did you call, Jake?"

He sighed. "Now that you know who you are and what's going on, I want to keep you updated on what's happening with the investigation."

Did she want to know any more than she already did? All her life she'd wondered about where she came from, what her life had been like before the Martins had adopted her, and now she knew more than she cared to know. "What is it?" She could tell, from the tone of Jake's voice, that what was coming would be big.

"There's no easy way to tell you this. I'm still struggling with the discovery myself." There was another sigh, a short pause, and then Jake continued. "In studying a number of previously secret government documents, I've learned that when Gretchen and I were born, there was a third child. We'd always assumed there were only the two of us, but…that was incorrect. We were triplets, not twins. Violet was told that the third baby died, but he didn't. He was born blind, so they sent him away." There was a touch of wonder and anger in Jake's deep voice. "He didn't die, Faith. We have another brother. Gretchen and I are doing everything we can to find him."

Another brother. Why was that news so shocking? In the past few days she had already uncovered three brothers and a sister.

Her fears about her past were not soothed by this news. A child of the experiment had been born blind, so the scientists in charge had discarded him. If she had been born less than perfect, would she have been discarded? She, her sister, her brothers, they had never been anything more than lab experiments. Perhaps the woman she vaguely remembered as her mother had loved them. Perhaps not.

She didn't want to care about any of these people...but she couldn't help herself. They were her family. They were blood. "What about Gideon?"

Gideon, a child who had shared a womb with Faith and Mark, the boy who had been left behind when the other had been rescued, had been presumed dead for many years.

"Nothing new," Jake said in a low voice. "I finally managed to get a meeting with the intelligence heads I told you about, and I did my best to convince them that Gideon, the man they know as Achilles, is not a criminal, that he's been forced to commit crimes. They were skeptical, but at least they listened to me."

"You told them about the experiments, too, and that we'd been—" the word caught in her throat "—programmed."

"Yes."

"Did they believe you?"

"I think so. Eventually."

Faith's fingers played absently with a dull pencil she found sitting on Luke's desk. Her life, what was left of it, was spinning out of control. Control was all she had, and it would soon be completely gone. "Did you tell them you'd found me?"

She held her breath until he answered. "No. And I won't, not until we can have Maisy take you through the process of deprogramming. I can't trust everyone. Some days it seems like I can't trust anyone at all."

To Faith's logical mind, none of this seemed likely. How could hypnosis force a person to do something, anything, they would not ordinarily do? She didn't believe it was possible, especially not when the supposed programming had taken place more than twenty years ago.

In Gideon's case, though, those twisted scientists Agnes Payne and Oliver Grimble had had a lifetime to exert their influence over an exceptional child who had no doubt grown to be a brilliant man. She wanted to believe that her brother was innocent of all crimes, but the truth was, neither she nor Jake knew Gideon. Not now. They remembered the child, perhaps, but they did not know the man or of what he might be capable.

All the money, all the good intentions in the world might not be enough to save any of them. She knew that. So did Jake, she imagined.

"I want you to call me before the quarantine is lifted," Jake said, using a tone of voice he probably called upon when he expected to be obeyed. "The minute I can get in, I'll have a helicopter there to whisk you out."

"Surely that's not—"

"Necessary? Of course it is," Jake snapped. "If I found you through the press coverage of this epidemic, then so did the Coalition. As soon as they can get to

you, you're in danger. We'll transport you to a safe
place and bring in Maisy to do the deprogramming.''

''I haven't been programmed,'' Faith insisted
sharply. She would know if anyone had done such a
thing to her, if the remnants of some evil experiment
slept in her brain. Wouldn't she? Wouldn't she feel
that something was wrong?

''Yes, you have,'' Jake said gently. ''Faith, you
don't have any choice about this. Neither do I. Until
the Coalition is stopped, you need to be on Brunhia
with Gretchen. You'll be safe there.''

She didn't want to bring her life to a halt, but already she knew better than to argue with Jake. It
would be an endless exercise, neither of them giving
in. But she couldn't keep herself from asking, ''What
if the Coalition can't be stopped?''

Jake didn't have an answer for her. ''Call me again
tomorrow and let me know what's going on,'' he said.
''I won't rest easy until you're safely out of there.''
He laughed lightly. ''I can't wait to see you in person.
And Marcus is champing at the bit to get to you.''

''I remember him most clearly of all,'' she confessed. Mark. He was called Marcus now, Jake had
told her.

''That doesn't surprise me.''

Well, it surprised the hell out of her! She didn't
admit as much. ''I'll call you in the morning, if I have
the time.''

''Make the time,'' he ordered in an insistent but
loving tone of voice. Jake laughed lightly; she got the
distinct feeling he was laughing at himself. ''Don't
give your big brother a heart attack. If I had my way,
I'd have you checking in every thirty minutes.''

''I'll call in the morning,'' she promised.

Jake took a deep breath and exhaled slowly. Belatedly, and not very convincingly, he answered her question. "Faith, we will stop them," he said. "We have to."

Luke found Faith sitting at his desk. According to Molly, she'd been closed in his office for over an hour. He'd expected to find her talking on the phone, or going over case files, or maybe even sleeping.

Instead, she just sat there, staring at the phone as if she were in a daze while she played mindlessly with a yellow pencil.

"Hi," he said, closing the door behind him. "Are you okay?"

Faith glanced up sharply. "I'm fine. Why do people keep asking me if I'm okay?"

He wasn't put off by her sharp tone. How could he be, when she looked so miserable? "Maybe because you look like you're about to pass out."

She didn't argue with him. In fact, her face seemed to fall. "I didn't sleep well last night," she said softly, blushing and lowering her eyes as she, perhaps, remembered why she hadn't slept well.

"Come on," he said, stepping closer and offering Faith his hand. "Let me take you back to your room."

"I can't. There's so much to be done, and I…I can't leave the clinic."

"The patients are all on the mend." He gave her a smile. "A couple of them are wondering why they can't go home right now."

Faith shook her head. "They can't leave. Not yet. Not until—"

"I know," he said. "I told them all they'd have to stay put for a few more days." He gave her a smile meant to comfort. "Even Tyler is asking when he can go home." Just a few days ago, Luke had been so sure the young deputy wouldn't make it. Now the kid was grumbling about getting out of here.

Faith nodded but said nothing.

"The patients are fine, the doctors who traveled here with you have been working in shifts, and the nurses have finally caught up on their sleep." He tugged on her hand and she stood. "Your turn."

She didn't let go of his hand, but held on tight. "Luke." The way she whispered his name reminded him of last night. Gentle, tentative...sexy. "There's so much I want to tell you, but I can't."

Was she talking about the virus? He didn't think so. Maybe she wanted to confess something more personal but couldn't find the strength. Why did he want her to trust him with her secrets? He could tell himself again and again that this relationship was about sex and nothing else, but the truth of the matter was, he wanted more. Much more.

"You can tell me anything."

She shook her head. "No, I can't."

He wrapped his arms around her and she immediately rested her head on his shoulder and folded against him easily, as if they stood this way every day.

"Are you sorry about what happened last night?" he asked.

"No," she answered quickly.

Luke smiled. "Good. If I take you home tonight, are you going to invite me in again?"

"I—I don't—"

He tipped her head back and kissed her, midstammer. If she was surprised, he couldn't tell it by her response. She accepted the kiss, relaxed, wrapped her arms around his waist.

He liked the way he and Faith fit when they kissed, as if every part of them was made to come together in this way. He remembered the way they'd fit together in bed, so naturally. So comfortably. Her naked body and his coming together as if they'd been lovers for years, as if they knew every nuance, every unspoken desire. As if the comfort they offered each other went well beyond physical need.

But the physical need alone was powerful, much more powerful than he'd expected it would be. Heaven help him, he wanted to take Faith here and now. On the desk, on the cot in the next room. Maybe both. He wanted to make her scream again.

"Last night was great, but it wasn't enough," he said as he took his mouth from hers. "I've thought about you all day. I can't get you out of my head."

"I know what you mean," Faith said breathlessly. "I've thought about you, too."

"Have you now," he whispered just before he kissed her again.

The kiss was great, for a moment, and then Faith stiffened slightly and took her mouth from his. "Luke," she said breathlessly. "This is not…we really shouldn't…" She sighed and looked him in the eye. "I thought last night would be…"

He laid his lips on her forehead. "I have a feeling you're not at a loss for words very often."

"Never," she said softly.

"So relax and tell me what's on your mind."

She took a deep breath. "You surprised me."

Luke's eyebrows lifted slightly. "*I* surprised *you?*"

She'd given him the surprise of his life, well into the morning.

"I didn't expect to come here and find…you," she said, sounding almost bewildered. "And then last night, I assumed one night would be it. We'd give in and get this thing out of our systems, and then we could move on as if nothing had happened, but…"

"But what?"

"You're definitely not out of my system."

It was a confession made grudgingly, he could tell. "If it makes you feel any better, I didn't expect you, either. And you are most definitely not out of my system. Maybe we should just quit trying to figure out what happened and enjoy it."

He slipped a hand up her leg, brushed his thumb against the apex of her thighs so that she gasped. She didn't move away from his touch, though. She didn't tell him to stop.

She laid her mouth on his throat, kissed and suckled there while he touched her. He reached inside her lab coat and cupped her breast. Her nipple hardened beneath the thin sweater she wore under the coat, and her hands began to move. Her fingers grasped, her mouth worked against his neck.

Here. Now. All he had to do was move a few things aside and he could be inside her. But when he lifted Faith in his hands, propped her up on the desk and spread her thighs, she tensed.

"What are you doing?"

"What does it look like?"

She blushed. "I got carried away," she admitted. "But we can't do this here, Luke. Someone might hear us. Someone might walk in right in the middle of…right in the middle."

"I can lock the door."

She seemed to ponder the proposition for a moment, and if he wasn't mistaken she considered the offer seriously. Finally she shook her head. "Not here."

"Not feeling adventurous tonight," Luke said, setting Faith on her feet and wrapping his arms around her.

She laughed. "In case you haven't already figured it out, I'm *never* adventurous."

He lifted his eyebrows. Faith looked completely serious. "Last night…" he began.

"Last night was an aberration."

"An aberration."

"I'm…not myself these days." She leaned against him.

"So, no wild sex on my desk. I guess I can live with that for now," Luke teased as he stroked Faith's back. "But if I take you back to the motel, are you going to ask me in?"

Faith hesitated, but her body remained relaxed against his. Finally she whispered, "Yes."

Sleep called Faith, but she didn't want to go. If she slept, she wouldn't be able to feel Luke's bare skin against hers. She wouldn't be able to sigh against his chest and feather small kisses there, feel his fingers in her hair, listen to the way his heart pounded as hers did.

Tonight they hadn't been able to get undressed fast enough. What had started in his office had ended right here. And none too soon. Even now she could feel her heart pounding too hard. Her entire body trembled, and she could still feel the way Luke had come into her.

She wasn't ready to let the memory of those sensations go, so she didn't want to fall asleep just yet. Besides, there would be dreams. She knew there would be nightmares of the past when she closed her eyes. Tonight, in addition to the visitation from the children Jake and Mark had been and the sister she barely remembered, she might dream of a brother she had never known, of another brother who had been lost to them. No, *taken* from them.

Much as she wanted to remain lost in this haze she and Luke had made, there were other things on her mind. She wanted to ask Luke about his late wife. She wanted to *know,* but the right words never came together. She played the possibilities through her mind a hundred times, searching for a way to ask without sounding either jealous or rudely nosy. How could she ask him if he was still in love with a dead woman?

No, any talk about her future or his past would ruin the moment. This was better, at least for now. She wanted to enjoy the fantasy while it lasted. Reality would intrude soon enough.

Reality intruded much sooner than she'd expected.

"Stay," Luke whispered.

Faith raised her head slightly. "What?"

He reached out and brushed a strand of hair away from her face. "When this is over, I'd like you to stay in Rockland. With me," he added, as if she didn't understand. "A week, a month…" He grinned. "A year. I want you here with me when we're not fighting for our lives every day, when we're not surrounded by soldiers and reporters. Stay," he said again.

Her heart fluttered. It didn't make any sense, but what Luke asked for was what she wanted, too. Night after night together. Long walks. Fishing. Dancing.

*Time.* Unfortunately, they didn't have time. And she couldn't tell him why.

"I can't," she whispered.

Luke's smile faded. "Why not?"

She wanted to tell him everything, and if she could confide in anyone in this world, it would be Luke.

But Jake had warned her, more than once, to keep this new knowledge to herself. No one could know the truth. Anyone who was brought into this fantastic intrigue would be in danger, just as she was.

The danger to Luke and his child alone was enough to stop her, but that wasn't the only reason she didn't want to confide in him. How would Luke look at her if he knew what she was? The possibility that he might see her as a mutation, as less than a woman, stopped her from confessing all as surely as Jake's warning did. "I just…can't."

Luke appeared to be hurt by her refusal, and she couldn't blame him. It had taken a lot of guts for him to ask her to stay; she could never be so brave.

She touched his face, his beautiful, stubbly, masculine face. "But maybe one day I can come back."

He smiled, but not quite as brightly as before. "I'd like that."

"So would I." She settled down with him again and drifted off to sleep, not as afraid as she had been of what her dreams would bring.

Again she woke late. And alone. Blast Luke's hide! How could he do this to her?

She'd dreamed once more of water and fire, and she could see Mark's face clearly now, as she had once known him. His face was so soul-deep familiar to her, she couldn't even try to remember him without tears coming to her eyes. He was called Marcus now, she had to remind herself, and he wanted to see her.

She wasn't sure if she wanted to see Marcus or not. Not him or Jake or Gretchen. Everything was going to change when these people came into her life, and she wasn't ready. Would she ever be?

Faith showered and dressed quickly, turning her mind from the changes to come to this morning's aggravation. Perhaps Luke thought it was all right to slip out without a word. To leave her to wake, expecting to find him there only to be disappointed. Well, they would have to have a talk about that!

She relaxed a little. Maybe Luke really did think it was all right to leave quietly while she slept. Maybe he thought he was being considerate. She would tell him differently, and then he would know that she wanted the opportunity to tell him goodbye and to kiss him one last time, when he left her.

She knew they weren't finished. Though there was no possibility of permanence with Luke—for her there was no chance of permanence with anyone—she knew he had not spent his last night in her bed.

Faith reached for her watch on the bedside table, and the five foil-wrapped condoms there caught her eye. Five? There should be six, right? She peered around the table and under the bed. Luke had probably knocked one to the floor last night, or when he'd left her early this morning.

She didn't have time to look right now.

Again Private Mimms was waiting for her. He greeted her with a wide, boyish smile. "Good morning, Dr. Martin."

"Good morning." It was indeed a beautiful day, bright and clear and cold. Only good things should be allowed to happen on a day like this one. "Did Dr. Winston send you here to keep an eye on me again?"

"Yes, ma'am," Mimms said. "He also said there's talk of snow and he didn't want you to have to walk or drive in it."

Faith tipped her face up and studied the clear blue sky. "Doesn't look much like snow to me."

"Not to me, neither," Mimms said in a lowered voice. "But I didn't want to argue with Dr. Winston. He wasn't in a very good mood this morning."

He wasn't? "It's been a difficult time for him," Faith explained.

"Yes, ma'am."

Had her refusal of his invitation affected him more deeply than he'd let on? She didn't have time to wonder why a man would ask her to stay, and then leave in the middle of the night. Apparently in a bad mood.

Jake was expecting her call, and she had work to do.

The crisis was almost over. She wouldn't be in Montana much longer.

# Eleven

Women had always confused him, at least a little. He suspected the fairer sex confused every man in one way or another.

But he had never experienced anything like this.

Faith arrived at the clinic, late again, with a sweet smile and an almost shy way of glancing at him. After last night she should not be shy about anything.

She had awakened him shortly after two in the morning. Bold, outrageously sexy, she had seduced him thoroughly. Not that he needed to be seduced. One look, and he was hers. All she had to do was smile or look at him sideways, and he was a complete goner. That confused him, too.

Last night in his office, Faith had insisted that she wasn't impulsive, but in the early morning hours she'd been wild. Uninhibited. Definitely impulsive.

When she'd finished with him, somewhere around three in the morning, she'd tossed him out again. Quickly and efficiently, and with another of those soul-searing kisses that drained his brain while she all but pushed him out the door. She needed to work, she'd said between kisses, and he distracted her. He had to go. She needed to be alone.

No wonder he was confused.

All day he'd planned to corner Faith for a few pertinent questions. No opportunity ever arose. There were a couple of times when it seemed she wanted to talk to him, too, but they were always interrupted. The second floor of the Carson County Clinic was not exactly a secluded place these days. This discussion would need to be private. Very, very private. He didn't think he could wait until tonight, but as the day wore on it became apparent that he might have no choice in the matter.

Faith made a few phone calls, visited all the patients and then spent the balance of the day in her lab. She left the liaison work to Dr. Gant, so she had no direct contact with the two suited government officials in charge or the major who commanded the soldiers keeping the town safe and the virus contained. She seemed more comfortable in the lab studying the virus than she did with people.

There were times, moments, when she seemed perfectly comfortable with him.

Luke saw uninfected patients in the makeshift clinic down the street and then returned to monitor those who had been infected by the virus. Throughout the long day, he never got a chance to speak to Faith alone for more than a couple of minutes.

Not nearly enough time to ask her what the hell was going on.

It was after three in the afternoon when Molly burst into Angela's room, where Luke was examining a much improved Benjy. "It's Debbie McCord," Molly said. "She's gone into labor."

Debbie was expecting her first child in two weeks. Luke had hoped the quarantine would be lifted by the time her baby came, but that wasn't going to happen. "Have Stu drive her into town," he said, as he stepped into the hallway. "I can get set up in the new clinic…"

Already Molly was shaking her head. "Nope. They're scared to come to town, with the epidemic and the soldiers everywhere and all. Can't say that I blame them. Stu and Debbie both want the baby born there at the ranch."

"Great," Luke mumbled.

"Stu said the baby could come any minute and you'd better get your butt out there pronto."

Babies knew nothing about timing. They didn't care about epidemics or a doctor's screwed-up love life. Luke glanced toward the window at the end of the hall and saw light snow falling. Apparently they didn't care about bad weather, either. "Okay." What choice did he have?

Molly followed him to his office, where Luke would quickly put together a bag of basic supplies to take with him.

"Tell Dr. Martin that I have an urgent need to speak with her, but it might be morning before I get back," Luke said as he placed his medical bag on his desk and opened it wide. In spite of Stu's insistence that the baby could arrive any minute, Luke had a feeling he'd be at the McCord ranch for a while.

His nurse smiled as she said, "I'll deliver the message. Urgent, huh?"

"What's the silly grin for?"

Molly perched on the side of his desk and struck a casual pose. "I'm not blind, Luke, and neither is anyone else. I think it's great, myself. One of her associates might not agree. Dr. Helm, the tall, friendly one with the blond hair. He's not too happy about the situation. I think he might have had romantically inclined plans himself, but apparently he was too slow in making his move. Dr. Gant and Dr. White are both okay with it. Apparently Dr. Martin is usually all work and no play, and the guys are happy to see her playing a little bit."

*The guys?* Too late Luke muttered, "I have no idea what you're talking about."

Molly didn't buy it. Her smile died slowly. "It's time, Luke. Time to get on with your life. I like her. She gets the official Molly stamp of approval, not that it makes any difference who approves when it comes to matters of the heart."

*Matters of the heart.* Yeah, like it or not his heart was definitely involved. What about Faith? Was her heart a part of this or was their impulsive affair just a casual fling for her? He would not have thought her capable of a casual sexual encounter, but the woman who woke him in the middle of the night with expert hands and softly spoken demands was not the timid wallflower Dr. Faith Martin normally appeared to be.

"You know," Molly said in a dreamy voice, "I was so worried about Betsy, but I think maybe Dr. White actually likes her. Did you ever talk to him? You know, about not trifling with Betsy's affections."

"No." Finding time to talk to Faith was a problem. Cornering one of her geeks for a dressing-down wasn't at the top of his list of things to do. He had a feeling nothing he could say to either White or Betsy would make a difference, anyway.

"Just as well," Molly said softly. "Maybe we should let nature take its course. Betsy's shy, but she's a grown woman. I should probably quit trying to interfere in her love life."

Luke glanced up at the content woman. "You think?"

Her response was a cutting glare. "Don't get smart with me. Hey, I've been married more than twenty years. The romance is still alive at my house, but it's not *new* anymore. There's something very energizing about romance when it's fresh. Let me live vicariously through you and Betsy. Well, you and Dr. Martin, and Betsy and Dr. White," she clarified.

"This is a fascinating discussion," Luke said dryly, "but if you don't mind, I have a baby to deliver." He snapped his bag closed and walked briskly past Molly. He left the office without looking back.

Snow. She had known it was coming for days, and here it was, falling fast in large flakes that quickly covered the ground in a blanket of white.

Luke had left the clinic a couple of hours ago. Molly said he was at a nearby ranch, delivering a baby. After everything they'd seen here, after all the uncertain days, it was nice to know that life went on.

Still, she missed him. Missed turning around to find him watching her, missed knowing he was close by…missed wondering if he'd go back to the motel with her tonight.

"Dr. Martin," Molly called from the other end of the hall.

Faith turned away from the window and the snow beyond. "Yes?" One look at the nurse's face and she was immediately concerned. Molly's plump face was set in a frown.

"Nelda's on the phone. Her sister fell and twisted her ankle, and she needs to get out there to help. It's pretty far out of town, but within the quarantined area.

With the weather taking a turn, Nelda isn't sure when she'll be home, but Luke still isn't back and Nelda doesn't want to take Abby with her. Her brother-in-law has a cold, and her sister doesn't like kids much when she's well. There's no crib or anything out there." Molly took a deep breath before getting to the point of the too-long explanation. "Can you spare me for a few hours?"

In truth, Molly was more necessary to the routine operation of this clinic than Faith was. Could they spare her? Of course they could. But it didn't make much sense to let her go.

"I can help," Faith said. "I'd be happy to take a look at Nelda's sister or—" Her breath caught in her throat, for a moment. "Or I can watch Abby until Luke gets home."

Molly's worried expression relaxed. "No one can handle Nelda's sister but Nelda, so I wouldn't ask you to go out that way. But if you wouldn't mind watching Abby…"

"Not at all. I'm finished here for the day, and I have nothing else to do with my time." But sleep, which she needed badly. Abby went to bed early, she recalled. Once the baby was in bed, she could sleep on the couch until Luke returned. Then maybe they could have that talk she'd been trying to formulate in her head all day.

Faith bundled up in her own coat and a snug, warm hat and boots borrowed from Molly. The boots were a size too large, but when laced up tightly worked very well. She asked a soldier to walk with her, when it looked like a couple of the reporters intended to follow her to Luke's house. Mimms was off duty, but a similarly fresh-faced young private accompanied her to

Luke's cabin, snow buffeting their faces and very quickly piling up on the ground. Her borrowed boots crunched in the new flakes.

The snow was beautiful, patches of pure white made bright by the lights of the clinic, a lone streetlamp and the light on Luke's front porch. She headed unerringly for the glare of that porch lamp.

There was something clean and crisp and hopeful about the snow. She rarely saw it fall so early, or so abundantly. So much of her time was spent in warmer climes far from home.

Faith's heart ached a little. In truth, she didn't have a home. She didn't stay in the apartment she shared with Janine long enough to call it a true home. She hadn't lived with her parents—her adoptive parents—for several years before their deaths. The house she'd moved into at the age of ten now belonged to someone else. It hadn't been home for a very long time.

She was beginning to remember her childhood home, the happy moments and the sad, the smells and the laughter and the tears, but that too was a home long gone.

Luke had made a true and lasting home here. He'd put down roots, claimed his territory, made himself an indispensable part of this community. He belonged here. She didn't belong anywhere.

Her guard for the evening was not as talkative as Private Mimms had been. He walked beside her silently, his head occasionally lifting to watch the snowfall.

"Where are you from?" Faith asked.

"Alabama, originally, but I haven't been there in years."

She smiled. "They don't see this kind of snowfall often in Alabama."

"No, ma'am," he said with a shake of his head.

"It's beautiful, isn't it?"

"Yes, ma'am, it is," the guardsman said reverently. That bit of polite conversation out of the way, they walked in comfortable silence.

No wonder Luke loved living here! The mountains, the magnificent trees, the streams where he liked to fish. He was surrounded by nature at its wildest and most beautiful.

In spite of their slowed step, thanks to the snow, they reached the cabin quickly. "Thank you for walking with me," Faith said as she stepped onto the porch steps. Jake's words of warning echoed in her brain, but she pushed them aside. She couldn't wonder about prying eyes in the dark of night, strangers lurking in the shadows. Right now she was much more worried about what Luke would think when he found out who she was. *What* she was.

Nelda threw open the front door as Faith reached for the doorbell.

"Thank goodness." Abby's nanny was already wearing her own coat, boots and scarf. "You're an angel to do this."

"No, really," Faith said as she stepped into the warm house. A low fire burned in the fireplace, and something aromatic drifted from the kitchen and teased her nose. "I'm happy to help."

A few minutes later, Nelda exited through the kitchen door and into the garage, where her car waited. She issued instructions as she walked briskly. Faith took it all in. Food. Milk. Diapers. Bedtime. There was an empty space in the garage, where Luke's SUV was normally parked.

Moments later, Faith and Abby were alone.

Abby sat on the kitchen floor with a collection of colorful plastic blocks before her. Faith waited for the child to start to cry. After all, they were practically strangers. But Abby did not cry. She studied Faith carefully, perhaps critically, but she didn't wail. She didn't even tear up. Good.

Faith removed her coat and borrowed hat and hung them on a peg by the kitchen door. That done, she sat on the floor with Abby, cross-legged and nervous. Why on earth did a small child make her nervous? Faith wanted Abby to like her. Normally she didn't care if people liked her or not.

Faith picked up a red block and then a blue one. Abby reached for yellow, and together they constructed a small stack of blocks. With a sigh, Faith relaxed. So far, so good.

"You look very much like your father," Faith said as she placed the red block atop the blue one. Baby talk was silly and unnecessary. A child would learn to speak much more quickly if he or she were spoken to in a normal tone of voice.

Abby answered with a goo.

"He's a very nice man, and I'm sure he's an excellent father," Faith continued. "This past year has been difficult for you both, I imagine, though you of course don't understand."

Abby glanced up with wide, innocent blue eyes. Luke's eyes.

Faith sighed. "You have no idea what I'm saying, do you. Would you like something to eat?"

The baby's face lit up, and she smiled and dropped her blocks. "Eeee!"

"Yes, it's time to eat."

Faith placed Abby in the high chair and affixed the large bib that had been placed on the table. She didn't see the reasoning in attaching such a large bib to such a small child, but since it was there she made use of it.

Abby banged a block on the tray of her high chair while Faith heated the child's dinner to the proper temperature.

As Nash would say, piece of cake.

Debbie McCord was healthy, and the delivery of her child was progressing normally. But this was her first baby, and things were not moving along quickly.

Stu, the father-to-be, paced restlessly behind Luke as Debbie silently suffered another contraction. "Isn't it about time?" Stu asked. "Can't you do something to hurry things along? What the hell is taking so long?"

The three of them were crowded into a small bedroom, and the impatient father was getting on Luke's already tattered nerves. When he'd packed his bag, he should have thought to throw in some sedatives for the new father.

"Everything is progressing very well," Luke said calmly when Debbie's contraction was finished and she breathed normally again. "Could you make me some coffee, Stu?"

Stu stopped pacing. "You want me to leave the room?"

"Just to make coffee. I promise you the baby won't

come before you get back. We've got a couple more hours at least.''

''A couple more hours?'' Stu asked loudly. Then with a grumble he left the room.

Debbie gave Luke a pale, wan smile. ''Don't be mad at Stu. He's just anxious.''

Luke smiled and patted Debbie's hand. ''I'm not mad. I understand exactly what he's going through.''

''I guess you do,'' Debbie said softly, closing her eyes and taking a moment to relax.

He'd delivered a lot of babies, including Abby. He remembered so well the night Abby had been born. All along he'd assured Karen and Molly and everyone else that he was fine. That delivering his own child was no different than delivering any other baby.

He'd been lying through his teeth. Man, he had been so scared that night. So worried that something might go wrong. Of course, everything had been just fine, as it would be tonight.

In the distance, a telephone rang. The bedroom extension had practically rung off the hook before Luke had ordered it disconnected. Everyone was anxious about Debbie's baby being born at home and wanted to know how things were going, but she didn't need to go through labor with the phone jangling beside her head. Anyone who wanted to could leave a message on their machine.

The phone only rang twice. A few moments later, the bedroom door opened and Stu stuck his head in. ''That was Molly.''

Luke's first thought was of Faith. ''Is everything all right at the clinic?''

''Yeah, I guess. She said to tell you that Nelda had

to run out to her sister's, and that Dr. Martin is sitting with Abby.''

Luke glanced sharply over his shoulder. "She is? Dr. Martin is baby-sitting?"

"Yeah, isn't that okay? I can call—"

"No, that's fine," Luke said in a calmer voice. Fine but unexpected. Faith, taking care of the baby? Somehow he couldn't see it. She'd been anxious around Abby that one night he'd taken her home for supper. Faith was as much a scientist as she was a doctor. She was certainly not accustomed to taking care of babies.

A mental picture filled his mind—Faith, rocking Abby beside the fire. Faith smiling, Abby contented. The two girls he cared for so much safe and happy and together. Warm, in spite of the snow. Happy, in spite of the crisis that was tearing this town apart.

Of course, he imagined no one had called Faith a *girl* since she'd been Abby's age. She was a woman, through and through, much too staid and sensible to be labeled a girl. And Abby was rarely content and quiet at the same time, so that part of the picture didn't work, either.

Nevertheless…he supposed it was possible. Since the image soothed him, he held on to it as Debbie's labor continued with a contraction that made her scream.

# Twelve

Faith glanced down at the splatters of mashed carrot that splayed across her blue sweater. "I didn't realize the bib was intended for *me*," she said softly.

As if she understood, Abby laughed.

Once again, Faith tried to lead the small spoonful of carrots into Abby's mouth, and again Abby pursed her lips and blew, effectively giving Faith a baby raspberry. More carrot puree flew in Faith's direction. Her face took the brunt of the assault this time around.

The child continued to reach for the spoon Faith held, but thus far Faith had refused to relinquish control. After all, the child would make a mess if she were allowed to feed herself. Faith glanced down at her sweater and sighed. How much worse could it get?

"Fine," she said, handing Abby the spoon.

Delighted and smug, the baby took the spoon awkwardly. Her concentration was intense as she scooped up some of the carrots and led the utensil to her mouth. The spoon took a dangerous turn and a small glob of the carrots fell. But some food clung to the baby-sized utensil and found its way into Abby's mouth. Success.

"Stubbornness is not an attractive trait in a young lady," Faith said sensibly as Abby continued to feed herself. On Abby's small plastic plate sat a pile of pureed meat, as well as mashed green beans and the infamous carrots. Abby didn't eat much of the meat, but she did take a taste. The meat went into Abby's mouth, but most of it was expelled with a small pink tongue. When Faith tried to encourage the child to eat more meat, she got a look that said, very clearly, "*You* eat it."

She did, reaching out to scoop a small bit onto the end of her finger and then tasting. No wonder Abby didn't eat the meat! It was awful. "All right," Faith conceded. "You can be a vegetarian tonight."

Her own stomach growled, and she glanced toward the stove. One pot simmered there, steaming lightly and filling the kitchen with a fabulous aroma. Stew or chili or soup filled that pot, she imagined, the perfect meal for a snowy evening. Faith was tempted to fix herself a bowl now, since Abby was feeding herself, but she decided to wait. Once Abby was asleep, then she'd eat in peace.

Tired of wrangling with the spoon, Abby began to eat with her hands.

Faith now knew what the bib was for. It was large, yes, but not quite large enough. Abby got more food on herself and the bib than she did in her mouth. Her cheeks, neck, hands, arms, even her ears were smeared with tiny bits of the gooey meal. Abby also managed to flick more food in Faith's direction. The gummy bombs usually landed when Faith least expected them.

"Your father is going to come home and find me covered in your food," Faith said. "He'll think I'm completely incompetent. Really, Abby, you must be more—" a lump of the tasteless pureed meat found its way from Abby's spoon to Faith's forehead, where it landed with a plop and hung precariously "—careful."

Abby smiled, again with an angelic expression that disguised devilish tendencies.

Faith wiped the baby food from her forehead. "If it wasn't so cold out, I'd suggest we move into the backyard and hose ourselves down," Faith muttered. "As it is, I fear we are both going to need a bath before the evening is over."

"Baaa!" Abby shouted with glee, slapping her hand down onto the tray with such force that a small amount of mashed green bean splattered out in all directions.

Faith glanced down at the spots of green along the splatters of orange on her sweater. Lovely.

Baby girl McCord was born without difficulty at 9:27 p.m. Debbie and Stu decided to name her Hope. Luke thought it a fitting and heartwarming name, given the circumstances. They could all use a little hope in their lives these days.

Although Hope was healthy and Debbie was doing well, Luke didn't want to dump the baby in her mother's arms and run. The snow was really coming down, but he had four-wheel drive and was accustomed to driving in these conditions. He wanted to rush to Faith and Abby, and he knew they'd be waiting for him when he did go home, no matter what time it might be.

Stu was in much worse shape than either his wife or his new daughter. He was wound so tight he was about to pop, and he was terrified that something still might go wrong.

"You're not leaving, are you?" Stu asked frantically.

"Not just yet," Luke assured the agitated man.

"Debbie's mama was going to come in to help, but with the baby being early and the quarantine keeping everyone out, I don't know what I'm going to do. I can't take care of a woman and a baby.'' Stu's eyes were bright with terror. ''I don't know what to do. You're going to have to stay.''

''I'll be here for a few more hours,'' Luke said with a smile.

''No,'' Stu said, shaking his head. ''I'm going to need you for a couple of days.''

Luke laid a hand on the new father's shoulder. ''Debbie and the baby and you are all going to be fine. I'll call Mrs. Langston and have her come by in the morning and check on you all.''

''Mrs. Langston isn't a doctor!''

''No, but she lives about five minutes away and she has seven kids and five grandchildren.''

Stu relaxed visibly. The fear in his eyes dimmed and his fists relaxed. ''Well, then, I guess she'd know what to do.''

''Trust me, she will,'' Luke said.

Debbie and Hope were both asleep, and Luke was no longer needed. Not for any medical reason, anyway.

But moments like these were the reason he had turned his back on making a career in a big hospital. He didn't want to run into a delivery room at the last minute, see a baby into the world and then rush out again. He knew these people, he cared for the entire family and he would care for Hope in the years to come.

Right now Stu was as much his patient as Debbie and the new baby.

Faith rocked the baby in the old rocking chair by the fire. The chair squeaked just a little, as a suitable rocker should, but did not have the desired effect.

Abby should have been asleep two hours ago, according to Nelda, but the little girl was wide-awake…and presently trying to climb all over Faith as if she were a play gym.

"Now, Abby," Faith said as the child grabbed her nose and pulled vigorously. "You know very well that it's past your bedtime. Think of how cranky you'll be in the morning if you don't get a good night's sleep."

She had tried placing Abby in her crib and walking away, after explaining that it was bedtime, but that had not worked at all. The baby had screamed in a way that was ear piercing and very disturbing, until Faith had relented and returned to the room to lift the baby out of the crib. At that point, the screaming had stopped with suspicious suddenness.

They'd had a bath right after Abby's meal, and the baby was now cleaned of the remnants of her dinner and dressed in an adorable pink sleeper. Faith had been forced to discard her own clothes. Not wanting to snoop among Nelda's or Luke's personal things for clothing, she had visited the laundry room and snagged a long, thick flannel shirt and a pair of too large but lusciously thick white socks. They were both Luke's, without a doubt. Faith's own clothes were in the washing machine, and if Abby ever went to sleep, she'd toss them in the dryer while she finally grabbed a bowl of soup from the stove.

*If* Abby ever went to sleep.

"You know," Faith said as the baby grabbed a handful of her hair and stood, pulling as she rose, "just a few days ago I was certain I wanted a child exactly like you. A messy, stubborn, disobedient child who would rob me of sleep and attack me with pureed food."

At this, Abby attempted to climb over Faith's head, using long strands of dark hair as her handhold.

Faith tried to keep a firm hold on the child and not lose any more hair than was necessary. "It would be foolish of me to have a baby at this point, especially since the child would have no father figure in her everyday life, and of course raising a child alone would be difficult." Abby giggled and muttered nonsense as Faith repositioned the baby in her lap and very gently rescued her hair from the child's grip.

"And then there's the newly added dilemma that there are apparently demented scientists out there who would love to get their hands on me," Faith said in a calm voice. "If I'm not safe, and my brother assures me that I am not, then no child of mine would be safe, either. Would it be fair to have a child, not knowing what tomorrow will bring?"

Abby cooed.

"This is strictly confidential," Faith said with a smile. "But I believe I can trust you to keep my secrets. You have an honest face."

Sitting once again, Abby reached up and laid a hand over Faith's cheek. That hand was soft, warm, so incredibly gentle. The smile that went with it was brilliant. Faith sighed. "Yes, it's true. No matter what the obstacles might be, if I had the chance I would love to have a child just like you."

Again Faith tried to convince Abby that it was time to go to sleep. The child was obviously tired; she rubbed her eyes and yawned sleepily, and occasionally tugged on one ear. Abby did not take a pacifier, and had finished her bottle a little while ago. Luke's daughter was charming and beautiful, but she would not listen to reason.

They continued to rock gently, and when Abby finally relaxed, Faith pulled the baby's head down to her shoulder. Where it stayed. "There now," Faith said softly. "Shh. Isn't that better?" Abby sighed and her body went limp. Completely trusting, warm and soft and smelling as a baby should, Abby cuddled against Faith.

"Time for night-night," Faith whispered.

"Ni-ni." Abby responded. And then she cooed.

Faith cooed back. True, the sounds that emanated from her mouth had no meaning, but it felt right to answer in kind. Abby sighed, and Faith shushed the baby with incomprehensible baby talk.

As they sat there and rocked, Faith muttered nonsense. She jabbered. She made meaningless noises that came to her mouth for no apparent reason. She resorted to gurgling and more baby talk, and Abby responded. Long after Abby fell into a deep sleep, Faith continued to rock and whisper.

It was late when Luke finally saw the welcoming lights of his own home. The snow had stopped falling awhile ago, but the ground and the roads were covered with the white stuff. It had been a long, slow trip from the McCords' back to town.

Luke opened the garage door and noticed that Nelda's car was still gone. Which meant Faith was here. It was after one in the morning, so she was probably sleeping. He hoped she'd found her way to his bed.

After the garage door closed, he entered through the kitchen. The house was warm, inviting as always, and he saw the note on the kitchen table. *Soup in the refrigerator. Hope everything went well. Faith.*

Luke stepped into the main room, and there she was. Faith slept on the couch, curled up with an afghan and a pillow, her long hair loose and falling over her white pillow. The lamp on the end table at her feet had been left on. Because she slept in a strange place? Or because she knew he would return in the dark? Faith slept deeply. At the moment the dreams that had plagued her over the past several days were letting her rest. Good. She needed her rest.

It had been a long day, but Luke was not sleepy. There was a touch of a chill in this room, so he quickly and as quietly as possible rebuilt the fire. Faith only stirred once.

As he tended the fire he wondered—should he wake Faith? Carry her to his bed? Or let her be? It wasn't a difficult decision. Much as he wanted Faith in his bed, he couldn't bear to wake her.

After he checked on Abby, asleep in her crib, Luke sat in his recliner, lost in shadows, and watched Faith sleep. The firelight flickered, lighting her face clearly for him. Heaven above, she was beautiful, much more beautiful than he'd thought her to be when he first met her. More than that, she was passionate, she was smart…and no matter what he said or did, she wouldn't stay here.

Knowing that Faith wouldn't stay, he should dismiss what they had as a casual fling and put anything and everything else out of his mind. They had no future, they had no past. All they had was today.

The problem was, nothing about his relationship with Faith felt casual to him. Anything more might be difficult. They both liked to be in charge and neither of them took orders well. She had her career; he had his practice and Abby.

He'd known Faith for a matter of days, but damned if it didn't feel like he'd known her all his life. Was it the crisis that drew them together? Faith's biological clock? Or was there something more pulling them toward each other in a way he could not explain?

Luke dozed off in the chair, his last sight that of Faith, his last conscious thought of her.

When he opened his eyes, a glance at the clock on the mantel read 3:17 a.m. Faith no longer slept on the couch. She sat at the desk on the opposite side of the room, scribbling furiously on a single sheet of paper.

For a moment, he didn't move. What a tempting sight she was! Faith wore his favorite flannel shirt and a pair of white socks, but her legs were bare. Long, untended dark hair fell down her back. Luke smiled. She was a vision, sitting at the little desk where Nelda paid the bills and wrote her cousins, wearing his shirt and socks and... Was she wearing anything else? Maybe. Maybe not. There was only one way to find out.

Fully awake, he asked himself another, less pleasant question. What on earth was she doing? The past two nights she had sent him on his way, insisting that she had work to do. Was this it? Did she often work in the middle of the night?

He stood slowly, and when he did, the chair squeaked. Faith jumped, glanced over her shoulder with wide, surprised eyes and held her breath for a moment. His presence in the room had startled her, but she recovered quickly, and while she continued to stare at him she opened the top drawer of the desk and slipped her nighttime work inside.

"I didn't see you there," she said as she rose slowly to her feet.

"Sorry. I didn't mean to alarm you."

"No," she said quickly. "I'm glad you're here." The smile she gave him was wicked and arousing. "As a matter of fact, I was just thinking about you."

Unlikely, considering the way she'd been concentrating on her writings. "What are you working on?" he asked, nodding toward the drawer.

"Nothing you'd be interested in." Faith took a step in his direction. "Nothing at all. You and I have better things to talk about than boring calculations and intricate formulas," she whispered.

Now was as good a time as any to ask her about the way she'd kicked him out of her bed and her room the past two nights. He had a feeling it had something to do with her boring calculations and intricate formulas. "Faith…"

She stopped in the middle of the room, reached beneath the flannel shirt she wore, and slipped her underwear down. She kicked the panties aside and Luke immediately forgot what he'd been about to say.

With each step she took toward him, she unfastened one button of her shirt. His shirt. She was wearing nothing but white socks and flannel and skin, and the flannel wasn't going to last much longer. Every movement was a seduction. The sway of her hips, the workings of her fingers, the smile, the way she tossed her head.

So why did he get the bone-chilling feeling that this was not the woman he was falling in love with?

"Faith," he began again. "We have to talk."

"We'll talk later," she said as she reached him. The shirt she wore was now completely unbuttoned, but she hadn't taken it off. It was opened down the front, and swung in a strangely seductive way as she reached for him. "Right now I have other plans for you."

She kissed him, mouth hungry and demanding, and Luke kissed her back. How could he not? Her body pressed against his, her tongue danced and teased. She laid a hand over his erection and stroked gently. "You know what I want," she whispered. "Here. Now."

His body said yes, but his brain was not yet convinced. "Faith, honey, are you awake?"

She laughed. "Of course I'm awake."

"You just seem…different." He took her face in his hands and looked directly into her eyes.

"I *am* different," she said in a low, husky voice. "I am Faith unleashed. I am Faith without inhibition." She unbuckled his belt. "Surely you like this Faith better than the woman who is afraid to look a virile man in the eye and tell him what she wants. A woman who hides behind her work because she's so sure there is nothing else in this wide world for her."

When she reached for his zipper, he caught her hand and stopped her. He didn't know what she meant by *Faith unleashed,* and until he did… "I like my Faith," he said.

"*Your* Faith?" She laughed. "There is no 'your Faith,' Luke."

"I thought there was."

She grabbed his free hand and laid it over her bare stomach. For a few moments she held his hand there, so that his fingers rested over the maddeningly soft skin of her belly.

"Your Faith is a more exceptional woman than you or anyone else will ever know. She's unique in more ways than you can imagine. She's strong, stronger than she believes she could ever be. No matter how badly she wants it, she will never be like other women." For a moment, Faith stood very still. Then she raked her fingers over the hand she held to her belly.

"This doesn't make any sense," Luke protested.

Faith laid her mouth on his throat, kissed and licked. When she was finished, she took her lips from his skin and moaned softly. "Can't you feel it?" she whispered. "Can't you taste it?" Her eyes snapped open and she fixed them to his. "Your Faith is a woman who cannot be denied, and tonight she wants a child. Your child, Luke."

"No, that's—"

"This body is ready," she insisted, "fertile and wanting. I can feel it tingling, calling out for you, demanding *you*. You have what I need, Luke."

He held one of Faith's hands, she held one of his. When she leaned in and kissed him on the mouth, it was with an open yearning he could taste. The unbuttoned shirt hung open, revealing more than it concealed.

"Only you can give me what I need," Faith whispered, "what I want, what I must have." She closed her eyes and took a deep breath.

"Not now," Luke said, his body ready to answer Faith's earthy demands, but his brain insisting on answers of an entirely different sort. "Not until you explain a few things to me."

She was clearly annoyed. Her eyes drifted open and she pinned her gaze on his face. "What do you need to know except that I want you? Isn't that enough?"

If this affair was as casual as she'd have him believe, it would certainly be enough. Sex for the sake of sex didn't require understanding. But since he suspected he and Faith had more, or at least the possibility of more, he had to push for answers that went beyond what her body and his wanted.

"It's your wife, isn't it?" she whispered.

A chill passed through Luke's body. "No."

"Don't lie to me." Her deep blue eyes turned hard as stone for a moment. "I've suspected all along that you still love her. I wanted to ask you about her, a hundred times I wanted to ask, but I couldn't do it. Maybe I was afraid of the answer."

He couldn't tell Faith, not here and not like this, that part of the guilt he tortured himself with stemmed from the knowledge that he hadn't loved Karen enough. Not for a very long time before her death.

"We're not going to talk about me right now," he said. "We're going to talk about you. What do you mean when you say Faith unleashed?"

She smiled. "It seems self-explanatory to me. The Faith you know, the woman everyone thinks they know, has hidden her power for years."

"Power?" he repeated. A prickle of warning crept up his spine.

"Power," she repeated, licking her lips. "Knowledge, yes, on an extraordinary scale, but more than that she has a connection with her body that no one else in the world has ever experienced." She kissed his neck and sucked, teased. "Can you tell me how fast your heart races when I lay my mouth on you?" she asked when she took her lips from his skin. "I can." She licked his neck quickly, with the tip of her tongue.

Luke's body responded; he leaned forward to answer in kind, but stopped himself before his mouth touched Faith's skin. Something was wrong, he just didn't know what.

"Blood pressure, heart rate, the slightest change in body temperature," she continued. "Right now my breasts are swelling slightly, just thinking of the way you will touch them, the way you'll feel when you come inside me."

"Don't..." Luke said hoarsely.

Faith lifted his hand and placed it on her breast. He allowed his fingers to linger on the soft flesh for a moment, before dropping them to her side.

"Have you ever been sick?" she continued. "Faith has not. Her immune system is beyond compare. She understands this in the back of her mind, and yet she does not completely comprehend what she is or what she can accomplish. She knows that she can monitor the smallest detail of the workings of her body, if she so chooses, and yet she suppresses much of that knowledge because it cannot be explained in a way she is willing to accept." Her tongue flickered over his neck again. "You taste good," she said in a lowered voice. "And you smell good. You smell as a man should—musky and sharp, like sex."

"Faith, stop." Luke did his best to pull himself together. "You're changing the subject."

"Yes, I am," she said with a wicked smile.

"I don't understand any of this."

"You only need to understand that tonight I am fertile. So fertile my body sings and shouts and cries for you. No one but you, Luke. My body has made this choice, as well as my heart." She sighed. "I do wish I could leave my heart out of this, but it seems determined to become involved. Such a messy complication, the workings of the heart."

Whether she was still asleep or in some kind of trance, Luke knew without a doubt that the woman trying to seduce him was not the Faith he, and everyone else, knew. What she had been telling him was mostly nonsense, the aftereffects of one of her bad dreams, perhaps. No matter how much his body wanted to respond to hers, already had responded, he knew he had to back away.

"In the morning, will you remember any of this?" he asked.

"No," she said quickly. "The mind denies what it cannot accept."

"What is it that you can't accept, Faith?"

She closed her eyes, smiled and took another deep breath. "Unleashed, I have unlimited power. Unleashed I am capable of anything. Everything." She took his earlobe into her mouth, sucked lightly, then drew away and whispered, "Unleashed I can create a child and destroy the world, all in one night."

# Thirteen

Faith woke not on the couch where she'd fallen asleep, but in a strange place. A strange, soft, warm place. One deep breath, and she knew this was not such a strange place, after all—it was Luke's bed. She was safe here, comfortable and content.

She opened her eyes to full light breaking through the wide window, to Luke sitting stiffly in a chair at the side of the bed.

"What happened?" Faith asked, sitting up straight. It was clear by the expression on his face that something was very wrong.

"Don't you remember?" he asked gently. There were circles under his eyes that told of lack of sleep, and those were the same clothes he'd been wearing at the clinic yesterday.

Something had happened while she slept. "Oh no," she whispered as she swung her legs over the side of the bed. "Abby."

"Abby's fine," Luke said quickly. "Nelda got in about seven this morning, right before the baby woke up. They're okay. This has nothing to do with Abby."

She had slept in Luke's flannel shirt, out of necessity, but suddenly she was very aware that her legs were bare. After everything that had happened, that shouldn't bother her...but it did. She pulled the heavy quilt over her legs and sat there on the side of the bed, facing him. "How did I get in here? I was sleeping on the couch."

Luke stared at her, hard. Clothes rumpled, a day-old beard on his face, eyes red rimmed, he looked rough. Faith wanted to drag him onto the bed, cradle his head and whisper nonsense into his ear, as she had done with Abby last night. She had an undeniable urge to make everything right for him.

"You don't remember?" he asked.

She shook her head.

Luke raked the fingers of one hand through his hair. Instinctively Faith reached out and laid a comforting hand on his knee. "Tell me," she said. "You can tell me anything."

He looked her in the eye again and laid his hand over hers. There was something very comforting about those two hands that quickly locked themselves together, fingers threading through fingers. His hand was larger than hers, darker and rougher, warmer and stronger.

"The two nights I stayed with you in your motel room, what do you remember about when I left?"

"Nothing," she said. "I was asleep. I meant to say something to you about that yesterday, but I never got the chance. You really shouldn't—"

"Faith," Luke interrupted sharply. "Just..." He released her hand and reached out to snag a piece of paper from the bedside table. "What is this?"

She took the paper from him. The notations, numbers and chemical symbols that were scribbled on the page looked like her handwriting, but that couldn't be. As she deciphered the formula—a portion of a more complicated formula, she realized as she scanned the page a second time—a deep chill settled in her bones.

"Where did you get this?" she whispered.

"I took it from the desk drawer, where you stashed it somewhere around three-thirty this morning."

She shook her head in denial but studied the neat handwriting. Yes, it definitely looked like something she had written.

"What is it?" Luke asked. "Do I even want to know?"

"I didn't do this," she insisted.

"I saw you."

Faith shook her head, then glanced at the formula again. "Luke, this appears to be a fragment of the chemical makeup of an extremely deadly inorganic virus."

"Like the one that was released here?"

"Deadlier. Much deadlier." She balled the sheet of paper in her hand. "We have to burn this." Had the pestilent specifications truly come from her head? Her hand? Dear God, how could she concoct something so vicious and *not remember?* "I don't understand."

Luke began to tell her a story she didn't want to believe. He held nothing back as he told her how on two separate occasions she'd awakened him in her motel bed, seduced him and then ordered him to leave. Suddenly the missing condoms made sense, and she knew that Luke had not sneaked out of her room in the early morning hours. She'd kicked him out so that she could create a virus that could be used as a lethal weapon.

She wouldn't believe it, not a word, if Jake hadn't warned her that the Coalition would use her in this way, if they got the opportunity.

Somehow the Coalition had gotten to her; they'd turned her into a twenty-first-century Jekyll and Hyde.

"How could this happen?" Luke asked. "How could you become a different person when you're supposed to be sleeping? Faith, do you know what could happen if the wrong people got their hands on that viral weapon you've been devising? What the hell did you mean last night when you told me you were Faith unleashed?"

She shouldn't tell him, but not only did she want him to understand, she needed his help. She could not be allowed to finish this formula, and without intervention she would.

Faith had to gather all her strength in order to continue. "I asked you once before if you'd heard about the genetically engineered children that were supposedly born in the late sixties and early seventies."

"Sure," he said, shaking his head as if he wondered why she'd changed the subject. "I remember."

"You said it was unlikely that such an experiment could have been successful at that time."

"Yeah," he said softly. She could almost see the mind behind those tired eyes working.

"As it turns out, it's not such an unlikely scenario. There was an experiment, and it was successful. There were children born of this experiment." Her heart climbed into her throat. "I'm one of them."

She told Luke everything, spewing the story out quickly before she could lose the courage it took to tell all. The experiments, the programming, the sister and the brothers she had forgotten and was now rediscovering in bits and pieces of damaged memory.

After the first few minutes, Faith turned her eyes to the window and the view beyond. She couldn't bear to look at Luke as she told him her bizarre story. He would despise her when she was finished, she knew that. He would hate her for lying to him, and he would be appalled to discover that she was the result of a twisted scientific experiment.

Faith's hands fisted on her lap, and she fought to make the words she had to say work their way past her tongue. All the while her mind spun in a hundred different directions. Her life would never be normal. She would never be normal. Most of all, it hurt beyond words to know Luke would never again look at her as he had in those early days. As he had just yesterday.

"Apparently the Coalition did get to me, before I came here or after I arrived, I don't know." She pointed to the crumpled paper. "This is the result. Somehow, I set aside the inhibitions that would normally prevent me from concocting such a formula and did this work in my sleep." She glanced into her lap. According to Luke, working wasn't the only thing she'd done in her sleep.

Luke said nothing, when she was finished. Nothing at all. What could he say? He either believed her story or he didn't. He'd either help her or turn his back on her. It was his decision.

"You didn't know it wasn't me?" she asked, her heart fluttering slightly. "When I...when we...you couldn't tell." She shouldn't be hurt by that revelation, but she was. A little.

"Last night I could," he said. "I looked into your eyes and I knew something was wrong."

"But before that," Faith said quickly, "on those other nights, you—"

"I could tell you were a little different, yeah," Luke interrupted, "and I was confused. But you woke me out of a sound sleep and I was swept away."

Faith lifted her head slowly. She couldn't live the

rest of her life staring into her lap or out the window. "A *little* different?"

Luke cocked his head to one side. "Don't look at me that way, Faith. It was still you."

"Not really," she whispered. She wished she could remember those encounters, even though she had not been herself. There wouldn't be any more nights with Luke. He wouldn't be asking her to stay, not ever again. She scooted back on the bed. "So, are you going to help me or not?"

"Of course I'll help you," Luke said, as if not helping had never been an option. "But we do have a few things to get out of the way, before we go any further."

Faith went cold. Of course. Luke was a good man. He would help her; he would do the right thing. But their affair was over.

"Last night you asked about Karen. My wife," he added quickly. "My late wife."

"Oh God, I'm so sorry," Faith said, bringing a hand to her chest in absolute horror. "I had no right. I never should've—"

"I'm not still in love with her," Luke interrupted, his voice soft but strong. "I will always have a special place in my heart for Karen because she's Abby's mother, but...I don't pine for her. I haven't been making love to you and thinking of her. She's in the past, Faith. Completely in the past."

She had not expected to feel such a rush of relief at that news. "I never should've asked," she said, her voice not as frantic as it had been the first time she'd apologized. "I am sorry."

"If you needed to know, you should've asked me,"

he said. "I don't want you to be afraid to ask me anything."

Poor Luke! Just a few hours earlier she had grilled him about his late wife and apparently begged him to make love to her. This time he had resisted.

"Last night when I tried to…to…"

"Seduce me," he supplied with a half smile.

"You didn't," Faith said quickly. "You could have. What stopped you?" Had he somehow recognized what she was? Had he been repulsed by her, even then?

Luke stood slowly, like a man who was bone weary, and moved to the bed to sit beside her. She recoiled a little but didn't push him away when he put his arm around her. "When we do make a baby," he said tiredly, "I want you to remember every minute."

"What do you mean, *when?*" she asked. He was teasing her. There would never be anything ordinary about her life. No husband, no baby…no man to love her.

"I'm tired," he said, falling back on the bed with her in his arms. "Can we talk about it later?"

"Yes," she whispered. "Later."

"Don't go anywhere until I wake up," he said with a yawn.

"I won't."

"Promise?"

"Promise."

Luke held Faith as he finally fell asleep, and she cuddled against him. He hadn't pushed her away; he hadn't called her a freak.

And he hadn't said *if* they made a baby together, he'd said *when.*

Faith drifted toward sleep with a contented warmth growing in her heart. He'd said *when*.

They tried to behave outwardly as if nothing had changed, but one aspect of their lives was going to be different, starting today.

Luke swore that he wasn't going to leave Faith's side, not for a moment. And he meant it. He couldn't stop what was happening to her, but he could watch over her. He could protect her.

He'd never been as scared as at that moment when she'd looked him in the eye and told him, in an insanely calm voice, that she had the power to create a child and destroy the world in a single night. The confession had frightened him because he'd recognized that she was telling the truth. That truth had kept him awake long into the morning, had kept him at constant vigil at her bedside.

A few hours of sleep finally behind him, Luke turned his mind to more practical matters. Someone here, someone who had come to town in the days following Faith's arrival, was with the Coalition she had told him about. They'd seen her on the news or read about her in the paper, and they'd come here to use her to formulate their deadly virus.

When Faith's nighttime work was complete and the quarantine was lifted, this person would try to escape with the formula for the new virus, and with Faith.

Faith decided not to tell her brother Jake that her programming had been activated. She gave Luke several valid reasons for keeping the news between the two of them for the time being, but he didn't completely buy any particular one.

Deep in her heart she didn't want anyone, least of

all her newly discovered family, to know what she was capable of.

They'd spent the afternoon at the clinic. Things here were finally under control, even though it was a much busier place than usual. Between the National Guard, Faith's team, the nurses and the healing patients, the clinic was full. Then there were the reporters who had limited access to the first floor. He'd be so glad when this place got back to normal!

Considering what Faith had told him this morning, he wondered what would happen when this was over. He hadn't been willing to leave Carson County for Karen. It wasn't that he hadn't cared about her wishes, he'd just been so sure she would eventually come to love this place as much as he did. She hadn't. She had died here.

He loved Faith. He wanted her to be a part of his life.

And she could not remain here. Not until the danger to her life was over. Would it ever be? Would she have to live her life on the run, hiding from the Coalition forever?

At the end of the day, he drove her to the motel. He wanted to stay at his house, to take her there and watch over her through the night, but she had insisted that they come here, instead. She didn't want to take the chance that Abby and Nelda might be exposed to Faith in her most basic and uninhibited state.

She didn't want anyone to see her that way, only him. Did she trust him that much? Or was he nothing more than a dreaded necessity to insure that the formula she composed would never leave the motel?

Faith tugged at the drapes to make sure they were closed tightly, with no slit anyone might peek through.

That done, she paced in a room that was much too small to accommodate pacing. She was nervous tonight, more nervous than she'd been even on that first night when she'd tried to explain away the awkwardness between them.

Finally she sat in the single chair in the room. "All day," she said softly. "We were together all day, and you didn't say a word. No matter how kind and helpful you are, I know what you must be thinking."

"You do?" He sat on the end of the bed.

"It must…bother you."

"A lot of things are bothering me today," he admitted. "Which one are you talking about?"

She glanced away before answering. "Me. You know what I am, and still…"

Luke left the bed, stood before Faith and took her hand. With a gentle tug he pulled her to her feet. "I know *who* you are."

She rested her head against his chest, and he stroked her hair. "I'm Jekyll and Hyde," she whispered. "And even after I'm deprogrammed, I remain…a Frankenstein. I will always be an oddity, Luke, the result of an experiment that never should've taken place. I'm not…I'm not real."

Luke very gently forced Faith to look him in the eye. "Honey, you are the most real woman I've ever known. You're beautiful and smart and you care deeply for the patients who depend on you for their very lives."

"But—"

"No buts," he interrupted. "The only unconventional thing about you is the circumstance of your conception. That's it. You're a woman, not an oddity. I know you. You have a fine heart, and a soul, and a conscience.'' Now would probably be a good time to tell Faith that he had fallen in love with her, somewhere between insisting that it was his clinic, not hers, and discovering that she had a deep, dark secret. He didn't.

She rose up and kissed him tenderly on the mouth. ''Don't let me sleep tonight.''

''I'll try, but you have to rest sometime.''

They began to undress each other slowly, comfortably, as if they had a lifetime to do just this. ''If I don't sleep, I can't work on that damned formula and I can't…be different with you.''

''I can handle whatever happens after you go to sleep, Faith.''

''Can you?'' They fell onto the bed, and he kissed her. Deep. Long. Her legs entwined with his and their bodies aligned perfectly. Faith's hair tumbled across the sheets, dark on white. The mere sight of her—perfect pale skin, that hair, those eyes, her shapely legs tangled with his—was enough to make his heart clench.

''Did I ever tell you that you have a nice ass?''

Faith laughed in surprise. ''No.''

''I meant to tell you days ago.'' *A lifetime ago.* ''But at the time, I figured 'Nice ass, Dr. Martin' wasn't going to win me any points.''

''I'm not sure how to respond,'' Faith said, laying one hand on his own behind. ''No one's ever complimented my rear end before.''

''That's so hard to believe.'' He kissed her throat, and the smile he'd been wearing died. Faith affected him so much more deeply than she knew, than he was ready to admit. Luke brushed his nose across her throat and breathed deep. ''When I first met you, when you stormed into the clinic like a freight train and took over, I was angry and frustrated…and still I kept getting distracted by your scent. I love the way you smell, Faith. I've always loved the way you smell.''

''Of the five senses, the sense of smell is the most primitive,'' she informed him. ''It's—''

''No lectures,'' Luke interrupted. ''Not tonight.'' He kissed her throat again, tasting her, becoming a part of her long before their bodies were joined. ''Just tell me. Is it perfume, scented soap, some exotic shampoo?''

''I told you I don't use perfume,'' she said softly. ''And I use whatever soap or shampoo is handy.''

He lifted his head and stared down at her. Maybe she was right. Maybe he was drawn to her on a primal level that could not be explained. He recognized her as his, in a way that could not be defined.

She smiled widely and raked one foot over his calf. ''Freight train?''

''Yeah.'' He returned her easy smile. ''Freight train.''

Faith shifted her body slightly so that it rubbed against his in interesting ways. ''I suppose I should be offended by that metaphor, but for some reason I'm not.''

There was more truth to the comparison than Luke wanted to let on. Faith hadn't just barreled into his clinic and his town, she had made an absolute wreck of his personal life, such as it was. She made him question everything; she made him want things he had given up on long ago. Things he had given up on years before Karen's death.

Faith's hand drifted lazily down his side and rested on his hip, and then she threaded her fingers through his hair and pulled his mouth to hers. There was no more talk as they kissed and touched and their minds were cleared of everything but sensation and love. He still didn't say it, and neither did she, but the love was there.

After a while, Faith reached out and snagged a condom from the bedside table. Last night, when she'd been without inhibition, she had insisted that he come to her without anything between them, but tonight she obviously felt differently.

"I thought you wanted a baby," he said as he took the foil-wrapped protection from her.

"I do," she said, kissing him again. "Heaven help me, I do, more than you'll ever know. But how can I even think of bringing a child into the world when I don't know who I am or what will happen next? A baby of mine would be in as much danger as I am, and you..."

"What about me?" he asked when she hesitated.

Faith laid her hand on his face, traced his jaw with a delicate finger. "I shouldn't drag you into my life in any way. You shouldn't be here now. I shouldn't...care about you. Anyone who's close to me is in danger, Luke. Real physical danger. My child, the father of my child...they wouldn't be safe."

Luke opened the package and sheathed himself quickly, then rolled Faith onto her back. "You can't live your whole life looking over your shoulder, waiting for the bad guys to show up."

"What choice do I have?" she asked breathlessly.

None, he imagined. He kissed Faith again, wiping away the talk of dangers they could not see or control. She closed her eyes and held on tight, perfectly willing to be swept away by physical sensation and the tenuous emotional connection that bound them together.

He entered her slowly, and she moved against him with a gentle undulation that urged him deeper. She held on to him with her arms and her legs as he buried himself in her.

Words of caution meant nothing. He was already a part of Faith's life, and he wasn't going to undo what had been done. Not now, not ever.

Here and now, nothing mattered but her body and his. The comfort and pleasure they gave each other. The heat they generated when they touched.

As he lost himself inside her, he forgot everything else. When Faith shattered around him and whispered his name while her breath caught in her throat, Luke drove deep and found his own release. Their bodies shuddered and clung together, sweating and shaking, joined together in a way that went beyond the body. The words Luke hadn't said in so long, words he'd never thought to say again, teased his brain and the tip of his tongue. *I love you.*

There were very real dangers in the world that had nothing to do with the Coalition.

# Fourteen

Luke tried to stay awake, and so did Faith, but they were exhausted. Physically, mentally, they had been drained. They eventually drifted off to sleep.

When Luke opened his eyes, he saw Faith sitting at the small round table near the window, scribbling furiously. The lamp above the table burned bright, bathing her work space and Faith herself in harsh light. Luke didn't move, didn't jump up and try to stop her even though that was his first instinct. He'd watch, discover where she hid the notes, and then he'd destroy them.

Faith was so intent on her work, she didn't know he watched. Tonight—this morning—she hadn't awakened him as she had the other two nights he'd spent here. She knew it wouldn't be so easy to get rid of him tonight; she knew he wouldn't leave her alone, not now. Maybe she was hoping he'd sleep through the entire episode.

She had been naked when she'd fallen asleep in his arms, and she was naked now. Like a modern-day Lady Godiva, covered by nothing but her long hair, she worked mindlessly on her formula.

With the chill in the air, Faith had to be cold. Luke wanted to go to her, cover her with a blanket, protect her from the cold and the Coalition and everything else.

The demons he'd tried to bury for the past ten
months whispered in his ear. Who was he kidding? He
couldn't protect Faith. He could try, but in the end
he'd fail, just as he'd failed to save Karen. He could
love Faith. Dammit, he did love her. But was that love
enough? Faith was an extraordinary woman who deserved so much more than he could ever offer. Was
that what had kept him from telling her how he felt?
Fear that he wasn't ever going to be good enough for
her?

He hadn't been enough for his wife. She'd always
wanted more. More money, more prestige. She'd
never been satisfied. But Faith wasn't Karen. They
were nothing alike, not in appearance or personality
or in the way he loved them.

Of course, there was no one quite like Faith, and
there never would be.

Faith truly could destroy the world if she wanted to.
She had the power in her mind to do so many things.
She had chosen to do only good with her exceptional
knowledge, but what if for some reason she turned her
mind in another direction?

The Coalition she talked about could do a lot of
damage if they got their hands on her and had her in
their complete control. No wonder she was afraid.

There were moments when he was sure they'd be
together forever, that he couldn't bear to let her go.
She seemed to feel the same way, but was that just
wishful thinking on his part and desperation on hers?

He'd always hated the very idea of leaving Rockland, but that might be the only way to save Faith. He
had to get her out of town, as far away from this place
as possible. Maybe then she'd be safe. That was what
he wanted more than anything—Faith's safety. Her

happiness. She needed to somehow rediscover the peace of mind she'd enjoyed before she'd learned of her origins and the Coalition. Was that possible?

After an hour or so Faith finished her work, stretched her arms over her head and stood. She turned off the lamp she'd worked by, which left the room dimly lit by the bathroom light. Papers in hand, she walked to the closet and reached up to the top shelf. She moved an extra pillow aside and placed her work there, where it was hidden from view. From a hanger in that same closet, she snagged a red sweater.

Did she grab the sweater because she was cold? No. She didn't pull it on, but walked to the window and placed the red garment there on the windowsill, so it could be seen from the parking lot. Obviously, this was some sort of signal. Did that mean the formula was finished?

Faith returned to bed, moving slowly. Luke closed his eyes as she crawled under the covers with him, scooting close and aligning her body to his. Yes, she was cold. Her skin was chilled, her hands icy. A slight tremble passed through her body, shoulder to thigh. Luke felt that telling shudder, wanted to hug her tight and chase all the fears and the chill away.

He didn't. If he let Faith know he was awake, the part of her that was under the influence of the Coalition would know that he'd seen her work, that he'd watched her hide the formula in the closet.

Faith sighed, laid her hand against his side and snuggled close. She found her place and settled in. Head against his chest, arm draped possessively around him, she whispered, "I love you, Luke," before going back to sleep.

Luke's heart hammered. Faith loved him. She

couldn't lie, not in her current unrestrained state. She had no reason to lie. With her life in turmoil and her own demons eating her up inside, she loved him.

Maybe he wasn't good enough, maybe he couldn't save her. But he did love her. For now that was enough. Love was all they had.

In the night, with Faith clinging to him, the last of Luke's nasty demons died.

The first thing Faith did when she opened her eyes was glance at the table by Luke's head. She sighed in relief when she saw three condoms there.

"Don't worry." Luke's sleepy, deep voice drifted to her ear. "You were very well behaved last night."

"Was I?"

He kissed her quickly, and then reached beneath his pillow. "But you did finish this," he said. "At least, I assume it's finished. You put a red sweater on the windowsill. I figure that's a signal to whoever is going to try to retrieve the formula."

She took the papers from Luke's hand. They had burned the portion of the formula she had composed at Luke's house, but that work was repeated here. Seeing the entire formula laid out this way, page after page of detailed instructions, chilled her to the bone. The construction and release of this virus would not only be dangerous, it would be catastrophic.

This virus was much more dangerous than the one that had torn Carson County apart. As a weapon it would be virulent, deadly and quick. Drop a canister in the midst of a city on a windy day, and within days thousands would be dead. There would be not only flulike symptoms in the affected, but pustules and rashes. It was the kind of disease nightmares were made of.

The disease wouldn't just affect those who inhaled the contagion. Unlike Rockland Fever, this virus would spread from person to person with ease. What she held in her hand would be the plague of the twenty-first century if it fell into the wrong hands.

Among the pages she found that she'd composed a formula for a vaccine. That elicited a harsh, ugly bark of laughter. Heaven forbid that the Coalition might become victims of their own weapon!

Would the Coalition use this formula themselves, or sell it to the highest bidder? Faith shuddered, horrified that she was capable of devising such a weapon, even in the recesses of her mind.

"What will happen when someone comes here to retrieve the formula and it's not where it's supposed to be?" she asked.

Luke shook his head. "They won't like it, but we don't have any choice. The formula has to be destroyed."

She nodded briskly. "But I might try to begin again," she said softly. "In my sleep."

Luke took her face in his hands and looked into her eyes. "If you do, I'll be right here to make sure no one ever gets their hands on it. Or on you." He let his hands fall slowly away, but he continued to stare at her. Calm, steady and solid, he was her rock.

What would she do without Luke? Where would she be? If not for him, she'd have no idea that she'd been working on this biological weapon. The Coalition would retrieve it. Untold numbers would die. On a more personal level, his presence and support kept her on her feet and functioning.

Faith sat up straight very quickly. "I have an idea."
She went to the closet for her robe first, drew it on
and belted it tight. Then she grabbed paper and pen
and sat at the round table by the window.

Within seconds Luke was behind her, peering over
her shoulder. "What are you doing?"

Faith continued to scribble furiously. "I'm assum-
ing that whoever delivered the trigger and is waiting
for the formula to be finished is a henchman, a Coalition soldier, not a scientist."

"Probably," Luke agreed.

"So they won't know exactly what they have until
it's returned to the Coalition facilities and a physician
or scientist studies what I've written."

"You're so smart," Luke said, placing his hand on
her shoulder. Faith glanced over her shoulder to find
him dressed in boxers and smiling at her.

"It will buy us a little time."

He nodded. "What is that?" he asked, glancing at
the paper before her.

"Soap," she said. "The chemical makeup of
soap." She moved down the page and began to scribble again. "This is the basic makeup of the virus
they've infected this town with, with a few changes
that will make it ineffective." She moved to the next
page, and then the next, filling the white space with
harmless instructions. On the fourth and final page, she
wrote a lengthy paragraph. In Latin.

"What's that? I recognize a few of the words,
but..." He studied them with a frown on his face
while he tried to translate.

"These are very anatomically specific instructions
on what the bastards can do with this information,"
Faith answered.

When she was finished, Luke took the papers from her and placed them where he'd found the real formula. Then they burned the original pages in the trash can. As she watched the pages that held the formula for a deadly virus go up in smoke, a powerful rush of relief made her light-headed.

"You'll have to keep an eye on me tonight," she said, taking Luke's hand and holding on tight.

"I will."

"And every night until I meet with the psychologist Jake told me about and I'm…deprogrammed." Jake would want to know what was happening to her, but she wasn't ready to give up these last few days with Luke. And if Jake knew her programming had been activated, there would be no keeping him away.

"I'm here, Faith," Luke assured her. "No one's going to get their hands on you or your work while I'm around."

She watched until there was nothing left of the deadly formula but a harmless pile of ash. Only then could she breathe easy.

Luke flushed the ashes, so whoever came for the formula would not be wise to the fact that paper had been burned here. "We'll pretend to leave and then go around back," he said as he exited the bathroom. "I imagine someone will come here today to retrieve the formula. The quarantine will be lifted in a day or two. The haz-mat team is almost finished with their sweep through the county. Whoever is coming after this will want to take what they came for and get out of here as soon as they can."

Faith nodded as she grabbed an outfit from the closet. As she tossed the clothes on the bed, someone knocked frantically at the door.

"Just a minute," she said. Luke did not try to hide. It would be a worthless exercise since his SUV was parked out front. He stepped into a pair of jeans as she belted her thick robe tighter and opened the door.

Private Mimms stood there, oddly pale and sweating on this cold October day.

"Ma'am?" he said, swaying forward and grabbing onto the doorjamb just to remain on his feet. "I hate to bother you but something's wrong. I don't feel well at all."

Once again, the clinic was in turmoil. Half the soldiers who had been guarding the clinic had been infected with the virus. So had the blond reporter from Great Falls. The haz-mat team that had almost finished examining and cleaning every home in the area took over the first floor of the clinic and found remnants of the virus in powder form. It had been scattered near the area where the soldiers assigned to the clinic took their meals.

Faith was determined to save them all, and for once in his life Luke just listened and did as she commanded. If she had told him to go stand on his head in the hallway, he would have done it.

She knew what she was doing, more than anyone else ever could. And yeah, when she worked she was definitely like a freight train. No one got in her way.

By now she knew the virus well, understood its effects and its weaknesses. No one had inhaled as much of the stuff as Tyler had, so the cases were primarily mild. There were just a few serious cases, a handful that required Faith's personal attention.

Quickly treated with Faith's antibiotic, they were well on their way to recovery. Some of the initial victims of Rockland Fever were moved to Luke's make-shift clinic, in order to make room for the newer, sicker patients.

The media got hold of the story within a couple of hours, and the return of Rockland Fever was on every channel and would soon be in every newspaper. So much for getting Faith out of town quickly and quietly! She wasn't safe here; Luke knew that more than anyone.

Again Luke asked himself, why here and why now? Faith had been able to stop the progression of the disease in the original patients. She'd identified the source. What point was there in infecting the soldiers who were guarding the clinic?

Chaos. Whoever had done this wanted chaos.

It was well into the afternoon before Luke realized that whoever had planted the virus among the soldiers had probably retrieved Faith's senseless notes from the closet and was already gone.

A tingle of warning brought him to alert. Gone? Maybe. Maybe not. Would the Coalition henchman wait around to see if there was an opportunity to take Faith as well as her work? He knew that was what the Coalition wanted, more than anything else, even the new virus. They wanted Faith, and if they ever got their hands on her, they would treat her like a lab rat. They would use her as a weapon, dissect her, destroy her life.

No matter what happened, he had to stay close.

Jake Ingram called several times during the day, but Faith never had time to speak with him. Through Molly, Faith sent the message that she was fine, but she did not accept the phone calls from her brother.

Of course, Luke was the only one who knew Jake was her brother.

Another secret they shared, one of many.

When all the soldiers and the reporter had been treated and were in stable condition, Luke cornered Faith in the hallway and insisted that she head to his office. She hadn't sat down all day, much less had a meal, and he could tell she was approaching collapse. She was pale, and her usually steady hands trembled.

"Sit," Luke ordered when the door was closed behind them.

"Just for a minute," Faith said as she sank into the chair at his desk. She closed her eyes and took a deep breath. "I need to call Jake."

"Jake can wait," Luke snapped.

Faith smiled wanly. "I have the feeling Jake doesn't like waiting much, and no one ever leaves him waiting for very long."

"Too bad." Right now all he cared about was Faith, and she was exhausted.

"They're all going to be fine," she said. "Private Mimms was the worst. He must've ingested a larger amount of the powder than the others, or else his immune system is not what it should be. I thought for a while this afternoon that I might lose him," she said softly. "He's such a sweet boy, I just can't—" Her voice broke. "Sorry. I'm not usually so emotional."

"You have every right to be emotional," Luke said. "It would be a miracle if you didn't lose it now and then. You're only human."

She looked at him, tired and uncertain. "Am I? Human, that is."

"No more of this nonsense," he said gruffly, reaching out to take her hand.

She didn't respond except to twine her slender fingers through his in a gesture that was surprisingly and strongly intimate.

"You're the best person I know," Luke said truthfully. "Don't question who you are, Faith. You're the same woman you were when you arrived here. The rest of it…it doesn't matter."

"It does matter," she said. "And I'm not the same. I will never be the same."

Faith held his hand while she sat at his desk and composed herself. Luke watched her do her best to bury deep everything that haunted her. Her birth, her life, Mimms, the deadly formula she'd concocted…what was happening with them. She didn't speak, but no words were necessary. Sometimes just being with the right person was enough.

Eventually Faith released Luke's hand and insisted on calling her brother. Jake Ingram was not happy, Luke could tell just from listening to Faith's side of the conversation. She said no, sometimes quite forcefully and more than once, and judging by the number of her sentences that ended abruptly, Jake interrupted her on several occasions.

Faith tried to assure her brother that everything was fine, that she was safe, that everything was under control. She looked at Luke with quiet horror in her eyes as she kept to herself the knowledge that her programming had been activated.

He smiled at her, and she smiled back. Somehow he had to let her know that everything was going to be okay, one way or another. The virus was under control again, the deadly formula she had constructed had been destroyed, and she loved him.

She had admitted as much last night when she'd

been unleashed, when she'd been in that state of mind where she held nothing back. Would she ever admit to her feelings when she was herself?

Yeah, she would. One day. Maybe when all this was behind them and she felt safe again, she'd say the words again.

He was willing to wait.

Maybe he should tell her that he felt the same way, that he loved her, that no matter what happened they would be together. Somehow. Some way. Luke Winston wasn't a romantic who painted pretty pictures in his head of the way things should be. He knew what was ahead of them would be difficult, perhaps impossible.

He wanted to give it a try anyway.

Faith was busy assuring her brother once again that everything in Rockland was fine, just fine, when the door to Luke's office burst open and Nelda ran inside with a limp Abby in her arms.

"Something's wrong with the baby," Nelda said breathlessly. "She's burning up."

Faith slammed the phone down and jumped to her feet as Luke took his daughter from Nelda. Abby's skin was hot to his touch, and she wasn't breathing normally. Everything stopped for Luke as he looked down at his daughter. Time. Reality. The moment of peace he'd been experiencing a few seconds ago was gone.

As they ran out of his office, the phone began to ring again. No one bothered to turn back to answer.

# Fifteen

Faith's hands shook as she examined Abby. The baby was unconscious and burning up with fever. She knew the signs; Abby had come into direct contact with the greenish-yellow powder that was host for the contagion.

She didn't know when or how Abby had contracted Rockland Fever, but the child was much further along than the guardsmen she'd been treating. How fast had the disease hit the little girl? The very young and the very old were most susceptible to this sort of respiratory illness. At the moment, Faith could not assure Luke that his child would survive the night.

She'd dispatched a haz-mat team to Luke's home and had ordered Molly to begin treating Nelda with the antibiotic, as a precautionary measure.

Luke said nothing, at least not to her. He held his daughter and muttered that baby talk Faith had once been so sure was utter nonsense. Maybe she'd been wrong. Abby responded as well, or better, to her father's touch and words as she did to the antibiotic.

The three of them were in the room where Faith had found Luke holding Benjy on her first night here. The lights were dim, the baby bed empty, as Luke sat in the rocking chair and cradled Abby close. On her first night in the Carson County Clinic Luke had thanked her for saving the child's life. She had fallen a little bit in love with him then and there. Now what? If Abby died…

Luke lifted his head and stared at her. There was such agony in his eyes. "I can't bury her," he whispered.

Faith shook her head. "I won't let that happen." For the first time in her life, she promised something she might not be able to deliver. Abby wasn't responding to the antibiotic treatment. Slowly and surely, her condition worsened.

"If I ever find out who did this, I'll tear him apart with my bare hands." Luke's gaze returned to Abby. "I've never so much as hit another human being. I've spent my entire adult life trying to save people, not hurt them. But if I had a shot at the man who did this, I'd kill him. I want his blood, Faith. I want it for Abby and the five patients I lost, for Benjy and Tyler and Private Mimms and all the others."

*Blood.* A shiver passed up Faith's spine.

"Luke," she said softly. "I have an idea. Will you be okay here for a few minutes? I can send Molly in to sit with you if you…"

"We're fine," he said gruffly. "Go do whatever it is you have to do."

There wasn't time to explain. She ran, her footsteps loud in the hallway, from the room where Abby slept to the lab. She found Dr. White studying the newest tissue sample.

"Help me," she commanded as she stripped off her lab coat.

John was tired, as they all were, and the exhaustion showed on his face as he lifted his head and blinked twice. He pushed his glasses up on his nose. "Of course. Help you with what?"

"Draw my blood," she said.

"How much?" He walked away from his workstation and reached for a single syringe.

"We need to get set up for a blood transfer."

He raised his eyebrows and set down the syringe.

"No questions, John. We don't have time for delays of any kind." Faith took a deep breath and exhaled slowly. "My blood type is O-negative, which makes me a universal donor. Let's just do it."

Maybe her less-than-normal origins would turn out to be a blessing, in a way she had never imagined. If she was immune to the virus, as she was apparently immune to everything else, her blood might help Abby fight. She knew without a doubt that without extraordinary measures of some kind, Abby wouldn't live through the night. For the first time since she'd discovered who and what she was, Faith was grateful for the science and the experiment that had produced her.

Her blood could save Luke's child.

A strange man's arms held her tight and pulled her away. Away from Mark. Away from her brother. Everyone else was gone. *Gone!* There was just the two of them now, but no one would ever separate her from Mark. For the longest time she held tight to her brother, afraid they would try to take him away, too.

That fear came true. Another man tried to grab Mark, but that was no easy task. Mark was strong, much stronger than any other ten-year-old. He fought, and he fought hard. Until they came up behind him and stuck a needle in his arm and he went limp.

Faith's world crashed in around her as her brother crumpled. She had never seen Mark helpless before.

He was the strong one. He could fight anyone. If they could take Mark away, what chance did she have?

Faith's eyes filled with tears, so that the sight of her unconscious brother was blurred as they dragged him away. "No," she said softly, and then she screamed. *"No!"*

She woke suddenly, her heart hammering in her chest and the dream—the memory—still so real she could taste and smell it. Eyes remaining closed, she clutched the bedsheet in her hands.

It took a moment for her to realize that she was on the cot in Luke's office, and that he was with her. She'd come here after the blood transfusion. Tired, drained, depleted, she'd slept. How long? Molly had unplugged the office phone so Faith would be able to sleep. Apparently she had slept for several hours, she reasoned as she noted gray light drifting through the uncovered window. The night was almost gone. Morning was coming.

Luke sat on the side of the narrow cot, and as she woke he laid his hand over hers. The past faded, as it should after all this time, and Faith asked, "Abby?"

"Much better, thanks to you."

The relief that rushed through her made her light-headed. "You should be with her," Faith insisted, even though she didn't want him to leave.

"I stayed with Abby all night," Luke said. He managed a crooked, tired smile. "Nelda and Molly are hovering over her at the moment. They insisted it was their turn to pamper Abby for a while."

Faith nodded, glad someone was sitting with and cooing over the baby. She was just as glad that Luke was with her.

He lifted her hand and kissed it. "How can I ever thank you enough?"

"You don't have to—"

"Faith," Luke interrupted. "You saved my daughter's life by giving her your own blood. Don't ever doubt that you are special in the most wonderful way, or that I love you."

She didn't want Luke to love her because he was grateful.

But oh, she did want him to love her.

She scooted over so that her back was almost against the wall. "Lie down," she insisted softly.

Luke hesitated, but he did eventually stretch out beside her on the cot. Lying on her side with her face buried against his chest, Faith relaxed completely. It was nice to have him here, to be here. For the first time in her life, she was a part of something she could not explain. Certain phrases that had always seemed meaningless to her suddenly made sense. My better half. Kindred spirit. Soul mate.

"All my life, I've been afraid," she confessed. The last time she'd been with Luke she'd given him, and herself, perfectly valid reasons why she couldn't have a child. "I'm thirty-three years old, and I don't have anything in my personal life that could be called important. I have nothing but my work."

He wrapped his arms around her. "That's not true."

"It is. I'm tired of hiding," Faith whispered. "Not from the Coalition, but from life." She took Luke's hand and laid it over her stomach. She kissed his neck, then moved her mouth to his ear. "It just so happens that I am very fertile at this moment. My body is ready to create and nurture a child. Now. Today. How do I know that? I have no idea, but it's true. Bone-deep, I know it's true."

Luke drew back slightly and narrowed one eye. "Faith?"

"Yes."

"*My* Faith?"

She hesitated before answering, "Always."

"And you *will* remember this."

She caressed his cheek and the rough stubble there. "Most definitely. I'm not under the influence of any programming or hypnosis. I'm just tired of never taking what I want. It's time for me to take a few risks, to open my heart, to embrace life...and love."

He kissed her, his mouth coming to hers so naturally she knew this was right and true and worth every risk.

"Maybe I should work on being a little bit unleashed," she whispered. "Help me, Luke. Help me be the woman I should be."

He slipped his hand beneath her sweater, touched her in that way he had, the special, tender way that made her forget everything else.

Unleashed. No, she would never be completely without inhibition. But she could let go of her fear, while Luke touched her. She kissed him with an unbridled passion, caressed him without restraint. They belonged here, together.

They kissed and touched each other, their bodies pressed close on the narrow cot. Luke could never be too close; she needed him inside and around her, in a way that went beyond the physical. But the physical was fine. Very fine. They were both exhausted, beyond tired, emotionally battered, but the way they came together very quickly changed from sweet to demanding. A new and powerful energy chased away the fatigue.

When Luke slipped his hands into the waistband of Faith's trousers, she deftly helped him slip them down and off. Half her clothes were tossed aside, and without that restraint her legs wrapped around his. He reached between their bodies to caress her intimately; with his touch he made her shudder and ache.

She released every doubt, every caution, and lived only for sensation. Luke gave her that sensation, with his hands and his mouth, with the little moans that proved how much he wanted her.

When she couldn't bear another minute without him, she unsnapped and unzipped Luke's jeans, pushing them down over his hips. She freed his erection and stroked the length. Once. Twice. He spun her onto her back and rested between her legs, nudged at her center and then drove deep in one long plunge.

Luke made love to her in a way he never had before, harder, faster. He lost himself in her body. There was a newly discovered fire in Faith that she embraced with every fiber of her being. There was no fear here. There was only Luke. Luke and love.

Her climax was sharp, crisp, wave upon wave of pleasure and release. Luke came with her, gave her everything he had to give. Love. Passion.

Life.

Spent, he fell over her, cradling her body as he rested his head on her shoulder. This was the moment to tell Luke that she loved him. He was inside her, still, and she had promised herself she would be bold, fearless.

But some fears died harder than others.

Passion spent, the moment over, they separated and Faith reached for her discarded clothes as Luke straightened his. He glanced at her warily. "You're sure you're…"

"I'm fine," she said. When he did not look assured, she said, "And I'm me. Just me."

Luke grinned at her, and when they were both dressed he again sat beside her on the cot. "God, Faith. What are we going to do?"

She didn't know what problem Luke addressed with his simple question. He could be asking about so many things. So many dilemmas. No matter which problem plagued him at the moment, Faith knew they couldn't do anything until the Coalition was stopped.

"What did the haz-mat team find?" she asked, laying her head on his shoulder.

His stubbled jaw tightened. "That crap was all over my office at home. Abby must've wandered in there and…" He grew noticeably pale. He didn't want to think about what had happened any more than she wanted to face the truth. She wrapped her arm around him and held on tight.

Luke's home had been contaminated because he was close to her. Someone had wanted to get him out of the way so they'd have a clear shot at Faith, unguarded. If that were true, then the Coalition had the virus, had been in possession of it all the time.

No one who was close to her would ever be safe.

Another truth hit Faith between the eyes. "They planted the virus to draw me out," she whispered. "The Coalition did this because they knew I would be called here."

Which meant that the Coalition henchman who had delivered the trigger to her programming had been here in Rockland all along, waiting for her to arrive. Her mind spun. The trigger was verbal, Jake had told her that much. A nursery rhyme. Someone had to have found the opportunity to speak to her alone, at least for a few minutes, in order to deliver the trigger. Luke, his nurses, the people of Rockland, they had been here for years and couldn't possibly be associated with the Coalition…unless this place had been chosen for that very reason.

But then again…

"Mitzi," she said, stiffening and drawing away from Luke. "The reporter. I think she's the one."

"How can you be sure?" Luke asked.

"I'm not sure. It just makes sense. Luke, she planted the virus here knowing I would come. She planted it and waited, and she let those people die. More would've died, if the antibiotic hadn't worked. Abby could've died. How *could* she?" Faith began to rise, but Luke stopped her.

"You're not going anywhere."

"I have to stop her."

"I'll call the sheriff and have him detain her. If she is associated with the Coalition—"

"She is," Faith said, more sure than ever. "Remember that day when she spoke to me in the lobby, and I got dizzy? Later, I couldn't even remember what she said to me. That's when the dreams started, the dreams about my past. That must've been when she delivered the trigger."

Luke nodded. "You rest. I'll call the sheriff." He left her alone in the room, but she could hear and see him through the opened door. He plugged in the phone on his desk and made the call immediately, insisting that the sheriff find and detain Mitzi Chastain, but refusing to tell him why.

Faith knew she had to call Jake and tell him the news, too. He would know what to do.

She didn't make that call, but followed Luke into the hallway. He was headed to the sheriff's office; she was going to sit with Abby while he was gone. As he walked away, Faith muttered a very soft, "Be careful," and an even softer, impossible to hear, "I love you."

Luke knew the best thing he could do, for himself and his daughter, would be to put a little distance between him and Faith. She was trouble in a big way. It wasn't her fault, but to get involved with her now...

Too late. He was already involved with Faith, more quickly and more intensely than he had imagined was possible. He loved her, and he wasn't going to leave her to do battle with the Coalition on her own.

Luke knew his limitations; he definitely wasn't a fighter. He couldn't physically stand between her and the organization that wanted her in its dirty hands. But he could stand beside her. He could stay with her through this and whatever came after.

Sheriff Talbot had found Mitzi Chastain less than an hour after Luke's call. She'd been trying to make her way out of town on foot, apparently planning to trek over the low hills to the south of town. When caught, she had fought Talbot, but he'd managed to bring her in. She was now in his custody, locked up in the Rockland jail just blocks from the clinic.

Luke stood in the narrow hallway, sturdy iron bars between him and Mitzi. She sat on a hard cot, looked up at him and smiled.

"I won't be here long," she said confidently. "The people I work for won't allow it."

"The Coalition," Luke said calmly.

She smiled. "So, you know. It's a very dangerous thing, to be aware of the existence of the Coalition. You'd better watch your back, Dr. Winston."

He wanted blood, but not as badly as he had when he'd thought Abby might die. Abby was safe, sleeping in a clinic room with Faith at her side. Outside their door there was an armed guard who had strict orders not to admit anyone but Luke to the room.

"You almost killed my daughter," he said softly.

Mitzi shrugged. "Sorry about that. The virus was meant for you, you know. I couldn't even get close to Faith with you hanging around her all the damn time. I had to shake things up a bit, in order to get to her and the formula she put together for me."

"For you?"

"For me. Okay, it was someone else's plan, but I'm the one who pulled it off. Procuring that formula will secure my place in the Coalition. I'm moving up in the world."

"Doesn't look to me like you're going anywhere." He thumped one of the iron bars.

"I won't be here long." Mitzi seemed so sure she would be out of this cell, and soon. Her certainty was chilling.

She leaned back casually. "I didn't plan on you getting in the way. Everything was laid out so perfectly, but I did not plan on you."

"Did you really plant the virus here?"

Mitzi smiled. "The people I work for, they want Faith very badly. Finding out who she worked for was one thing. Actually getting our hands on her was another. I mean, the woman doesn't stay in one place very long, and she's all over the world. A few months ago another agent found out that she had been in a small village in Africa, but by the time he got there she was gone. It took him days to find out she'd gone to India, and by that time no one could be sure she'd still be there. One of the bigwigs came up with the idea to test the virus here in the States in hopes it would draw her out. Worked like a charm. We figured we might have to wait out another team of doctors first, before they called her in. Why chase her down when we could bring her to us?''

Thank God they hadn't had to wait. Faith had arrived with the initial team. If she hadn't, this epidemic might have gone on for weeks more. Months. Mitzi would have seen to that. "How many were you willing to let die in order to get Faith here?"

"As many as necessary," Mitzi said coldly.

He didn't understand people like her. Did the woman who called herself Mitzi Chastain have a heart? A soul? What about the people she worked for? They couldn't be allowed to get their hands on Faith. Not ever.

"What happens next?" Luke asked.

"Reinforcements will be here within hours. I missed my rendezvous, and that's going to set off alarms that will send my people running. Besides, I wasn't able to get my hands on Faith. They'll come for the formula, and then we'll move in and take her. By force, if necessary."

"The town is still quarantined."

"You think that will keep out the Coalition?" She laughed lightly. "No way. Besides, we've all been vaccinated. Even if some of the powder has been left lying around, the virus won't affect us."

People had died, and the Coalition had had a vaccine in their possession before anyone had become ill. Luke saw red all over again. "You'd go up against the National Guard?"

"A lot of soldiers are down with the virus, and re-inforcements aren't exactly pouring in. Things here are going to get really ugly before they get better."

"You're going to lose," Luke said.

Mitzi smiled too confidently. "I don't think so."

Faith lifted a squirming Abby from the baby bed and cuddled the child close. Abby rested her head on Faith's shoulder and sighed. The fever was almost gone, and Abby breathed normally. The treatment had worked. For the first time Faith was genuinely thankful for her origins. Her blood had saved this little girl. The fact that she was Luke's little girl should have made no difference.

But it did.

Faith sat in the rocking chair and swayed gently until Abby drifted off to sleep again. She didn't rise and place the baby in the bed again, but continued to rock.

It would be best for everyone if she just disap-peared. Today. Now. Luke and Abby would certainly be better off without her, and everyone in the clinic would be safer when she was gone.

The sad fact was, no one she loved would ever be safe. Jake assured her that Nash would remain under constant guard without his knowledge, though appar-ently the bodyguards assigned to her adoptive brother had already complained that he was difficult to keep up with. Nash had never lived by anyone's rules but his own. He was hardly going to start now, especially since he knew nothing of the danger to himself.

Danger caused because she loved him. It was so unfair. She could change her name, alter her appearance and find a small town in which to hide. No one would ever find her. Not Jake, not the Coalition, not Luke.

As tempting as that scenario was, at the moment, Faith knew she wasn't going to run. Not now, anyway. She wanted to meet her family, the family of her birth. She couldn't drag Luke into the morass that was her life, but she didn't want to disappear without a word, either.

It was too soon to know for sure, but it was possible she could be pregnant. The timing was horrid—a child at this time in her life would be a complication—but she could only be glad. She smiled, studying a sleeping Abby. If there was a baby, maybe he or she would look like Luke, as this child did. She hoped so. In that way, she would always have him with her. Always.

Luke had thanked her several times for helping him. She needed to thank him for teaching her to accept who she was, to embrace her beginnings as different but not monstrous. He had made her see that she was a woman, not a freak.

And she believed that he did love her, even though he'd only said so in gratitude. Still, she had sensed, hoped for and reached for love. That love had saved her more than anything else. More than any spoken assurances, more than any logical argument. She should tell Luke that she loved him, too, but that would probably not be wise. She couldn't stay here, and he wouldn't go with her. Would he?

The whirr of an approaching helicopter grabbed her attention. She had become accustomed to the sounds of helicopters patrolling overhead, but they never came this close. As it came noisily near, Faith placed a sleeping Abby in the bed and went to the window.

A military helicopter landed in the empty field to the north of the clinic. A single man, a large soldier dressed in fatigues and armed to the teeth, jumped to the ground before the Black Hawk completely touched down.

The soldier ran toward the clinic.

Reinforcements? Maybe. But why only one soldier? Faith stepped into the hallway. The private who guarded her door looked toward the window, and so did Molly, who stood a few feet away at the nurses' station. The other nurses were standing at the end of the hallway, watching the helicopter through panes of glass. It continued to operate loudly, its motor thunderous and the rotors whirring and whipping up a wind.

"Stay with Abby," Faith said to Molly.

Molly nodded and entered the room, and Faith ran for the elevators. Before she reached her destination, the door to the stairwell flew open with a resounding bang and the soldier who had exited the helicopter stormed into the hallway. He was only a few feet away, and his eyes immediately landed on Faith.

"Let's go," he said firmly.

Faith turned and ran. There were only two on-duty soldiers on this floor. The others were sick, in bed and unarmed. The two guardsmen who watched Faith and the pursuing soldier were confused, and rightly so. This man looked like one of their own, but he wasn't. He was here for her. She knew it. He was going to put her on that Black Hawk and take her away to God only knows where, and she'd disappear. Not in the way she had imagined, but in a much more sinister way. She'd be locked away, forced to concoct more deadly biological weapons. She'd be experimented on and tested and...

She didn't get far before the soldier caught her and wrapped one big hand around her arm.

"Whoa, Hey. Come on," he said, his voice surprisingly gentle. "You have to come with me."

"No! I'm not going anywhere with you." She kicked him in the shin, a wasted effort since he seemed to feel nothing.

"Listen..." he began.

"I have no intention of listening to anything you have to say."

"But I'm—"

"I know who you are, and I'd rather die than go anywhere with you!"

The soldier looked momentarily confused, maybe even distressed. Then he lifted Faith much too easily and tossed her over his shoulder. "Yeah, well, I'm not giving you that option."

She fought him as best she could, but resisting was like struggling with a rock. Nothing affected him, not her feet or her fists. The private who had been guarding her doorway stepped cautiously into the path of the kidnapper, but it was clear he didn't know what to do. He hadn't been trained to do battle with someone who looked like an American soldier, a member of the same team.

The last thing Faith wanted was to see the young soldier harmed, maybe even killed. He was no match for the Coalition henchman. She waved the guardsman aside, told him not to interfere, and then she again ordered the kidnapper to put her down.

Her abductor carried her to the stairway and held

her in place with one arm while he opened the door. He ran down the stairs so that she bounced on his shoulder.

"You can't do this to me," she insisted as he pushed open the stairwell door and burst into the lobby. "Put me down, you barbarian!"

"Look, I don't have time to argue with you," he said. "We have to get you out of here now."

"I'm not going anywhere with you!"

The sole guardsman in the lobby lifted his weapon, but like the private on the second floor he was confused.

"Lieutenant?" The uncertain private lowered his weapon.

The man who hefted Faith as if she weighed nothing looked like a friend, not an enemy. Again she waved the soldier back, certain that bloodshed would come of gunfire in the clinic lobby.

The so-called lieutenant stepped through the doors and into a cold wind, and he turned toward the helicopter that awaited them. Suddenly Faith saw Luke, less than a block away. He hesitated, looked directly at her, and then he began to run.

Faith continued to fight, but her struggle had no effect on the soldier. "You can't do this to me! Put me down, you…you…" There was no word fittingly repulsive enough for the man who was kidnapping her. "Luke!" she screamed. She tried to wave him off. "No! Get back!"

Luke ignored her order, didn't so much as falter. He didn't gain on them, but he almost kept pace. The soldier who carried her was fast, incredibly fast, even though he carried her like a sack of flour. She should be slowing him down more than this, but she was al-

most glad he wasn't affected by her weight. She didn't
want Luke to catch up with them. He wouldn't have
a chance against the soldier who held her. More than
anything, she didn't want to see Luke hurt. Or killed!
The man who carried her so easily was armed and
definitely dangerous.

"This is wrong," Faith said in a slightly calmer
voice. "You can't do this!"

"I'll explain in the helicopter," the soldier said as
he jogged toward the Black Hawk. "Just quit wiggling
around, Faith."

*Quit wiggling around, Faith.*

The voice that echoed in her mind wasn't that of a
soldier, but of a child. A strong, water-soaked child
who held his sister's head above water as he swam
toward safety.

Faith became very still and whispered, "Mark?"

# Sixteen

Luke ran as hard and fast as he could, but he realized with a growing sense of loss that he wasn't fast enough. The soldier, who was surely with the Coalition, was going to get Faith on that helicopter and in the air before he could reach them.

Suddenly the soldier stopped and dropped Faith onto her own feet. Above the thunder of the rotors, Luke heard the man shout, "Stop that!"

Faith turned and ran, heading unerringly for Luke. After a very short hesitation, the soldier pursued Faith. They all ran; Luke toward Faith, she toward him, the soldier behind Faith. The man who pursued Faith was faster than she was and obviously stronger. But since Luke ran as fast as he could, Faith managed to reach him before the large man caught up with her. Barely. The soldier was on Faith's heels. Luke grabbed her hand and forced her behind him.

"Run," he said, placing himself between Faith and the soldier. She grabbed onto his waist as the man almost ran them down. The henchman who'd come here for Faith wasn't merely large, he was solid.

"Run!" Luke ordered again. He couldn't hold the soldier long, but if he could just delay the pursuit while Faith made it safely to the clinic and got help... He realized with a sinking heart that he could only offer a short delay.

Faith didn't run to the clinic, but she did at least remain behind him. The soldier didn't attack, as Luke had expected. The big guy placed his hands on his hips as he ignored Luke completely and glared at Faith.

"You tickled me."

"Yes, I did," Faith countered. "You were always extremely sensitive between the fourth and fifth rib on the left side," she added in a lowered voice.

"Don't you ever tell anyone about that," the large man ordered.

She'd *tickled* him?

"You could've explained the situation," Faith said angrily, "instead of swooping down and—"

"There's no time to explain," the soldier interrupted. "Jake said to come and get you out of here whether you wanted to leave or not, so that's what I was doing."

"Jake sent you?" Luke asked.

The soldier nodded, answering Luke's question but keeping his eyes on Faith. "Yeah. What do you expect? You're talking on the phone, there's some kind of commotion. You hang up on him, and then you stop answering the damn phone." He pinned his eyes on Luke. "Let go of my sister. I don't have time for this crap."

"Mark," Faith began. "Marcus…you can't just drag me out of here. I have things to do. I'm not finished."

"Yes, you are."

Luke and Marcus echoed each other, and then their eyes met. They wanted the same thing. "You can promise me that she'll be safe," Luke said.

Marcus nodded. "Yeah. There's a place…I can't

tell you where I'm going to take her, but I can promise you she'll be protected.''

It was too soon to let her go, too sudden, but when Luke remembered how certain Mitzi had been that the Coalition would get Faith, he knew there was no other option. "Get her out of here. And once that's done, we need reinforcements for the ill soldiers. The Coalition is sending men in. Soon."

Marcus nodded.

"I'm not leaving," Faith held on to him tightly.

"You can't fight both of us," Luke said.

"Yes I can," Faith insisted.

Luke turned and took her face in his hands. "You have to go. The people who are coming here would do anything to get their hands on you. You know that. And you know what they'll do with you, if they get the chance."

Tears filled her eyes. "How can I be sure you'll be safe?" Faith asked. "If they've been watching, they know we're close. What if they try to use that against us? What if they try to use you and Abby as bait? I couldn't allow them to hurt you or your child in order to get to me."

Marcus leaned in. "I can arrange for extra security on your friends. No one will get near them, I promise."

Faith didn't argue. Maybe she knew there wasn't any choice for either of them, not this time.

There were so many things Luke wanted to say, but he didn't have much time. "When this is over, I expect you to come back." He brushed his thumbs against Faith's cheeks, wiping away her tears.

"It might be years before this is over," she protested. "It might never be over!"

Luke didn't have an argument for that, so he kissed her, tasting tears and desperation. The tears were hers.

Faith was right. They might never see each other again. But all that mattered at this moment was that she would be safe wherever Marcus took her.

When Luke released Faith, he turned his attention to her brother. Marcus and he were about the same height; Luke realized he might even be an inch taller. But Faith's brother was solid as a rock, a soldier, a formidable man in any circumstance, he imagined. It wasn't what anyone would call a fair match, but Luke wasn't going to back down. "You'd better take care of her, because if she gets hurt I will hunt you down and kick your ass."

Marcus grinned. Luke imagined the big guy had never been on the receiving end of any ass-kickings.

"I'm not kidding," Luke added, and the smile faded.

"We have to go," Marcus said, and Faith reluctantly joined her brother. He didn't have to carry her this time, but he did lead her along, holding protectively on to her arm as they approached the Black Hawk.

Marcus lifted Faith into the helicopter, and that was when she glanced back. Her lips moved, she raised a hand to wave goodbye, and then Marcus jumped into the helicopter and it lifted off the ground.

And Faith was gone.

The beach beyond the isolated house where she'd been hiding for almost nine days was lovely, the view from the deck that ran along the backside of the house breathtaking. South Florida was warm in October, and the sun shone down on Faith's face as she watched the waves lap against the shore. The breeze that rushed in off the water pushed her loose hair away from her face. It was a wild and free sensation, letting the wind flow through her hair.

She'd left everything behind in Rockland. Not willing to allow her to appear in public, Jake and Marcus had shopped for replacement clothes. The sundresses and shifts they had bought her were not her usual wallflower style. The dress she wore today was bright pink, and the barely there sandals were very feminine. It was not an outfit she had chosen on her own, but she liked it well enough.

The beach, the clothes, the sun, they were all lovely. But Faith yearned for something colder. She yearned for snow, and flannel, and flames in a fireplace. Most of all, she yearned for Luke.

Marcus assured her that Luke and Abby were safe. Once the Coalition had realized that she was no longer in Carson County, they had scaled back their plans. In a contained, isolated attack, Sheriff Talbot had been rendered unconscious, Mitzi Chastain had been shot in the head while still trapped in her cell, and Mitzi's effects, including the worthless formula, had been taken.

Here at the safe house, Faith had been deprogrammed by the psychiatrist Jake had introduced her to—his own sister-in-law Maisy. She no longer had to be worried about concocting deadly biological weapons in her sleep. She was still in danger from the Coalition, Jake assured her, but she was safe here. Isolated, guarded, safe…and lonely.

Knowing who and what she was opened a number of doors Faith was not quite ready to explore. When she closed her eyes and concentrated, she understood details about her body that no ordinary person could possibly comprehend. The knowledge came to her just as it did when she was working in the lab. She would stop, become still, and pieces of the puzzle fell into place. Only this time, she was the puzzle.

Faith now remembered a large portion of her childhood, and that included Grace, who was now Gretchen, Gideon, who was lost to them, Jake and Marcus. Her bond with Marcus remained, even after the years of separation. She could talk to him as she could talk to no one else. Unfortunately, he was very often away from the safe house. He came and went, here one day and gone the next.

Jake was also a hard man to pin down. They had spent hours talking, though, getting reacquainted and going over the details of the mystery that was their life. Her oldest brother took his newfound duties very seriously. He thought himself responsible for them all, responsible for the fate of the world and the effects the knowledge of their existence would mean.

There were so many unanswered questions. Were there other genetically engineered children out there? The Coalition might've managed to duplicate the Bloomfield experiments at some time in the past twenty-plus years since Henry Bloomfield's death. If there were children of such experiments, how old were they? Where were they? And what could they do?

Jake had rushed out of the safe house just yesterday, after learning from a government source that Agnes, Oliver and Gideon were believed to be hiding out in a remote area of Oregon. It would be tempting to rush in and capture the scientists who were such an integral part of the Coalition. And Gideon! If he was truly there, they might be able to rescue him.

But Jake was afraid to move forward until they knew where the other members of the Coalition were hiding out. They could be anywhere in the world. It would be best if they were all apprehended simultaneously. Otherwise they could disappear again, go deeper undercover this time. If everything did not go well, Gideon's life would be in serious danger.

Tomorrow morning Marcus would escort Faith to the island of Brunhia, where she would stay with Gretchen. She'd had time to get to know Jake, even more time to get reacquainted with Marcus, and tomorrow she would see Gretchen face-to-face. She looked forward to that meeting, but once on the island she'd be so far away. Luke would be completely out of reach, once she was on Brunhia. She missed him already. How would she function when he was on the opposite side of the world?

Marcus would return to Delmonico, once Faith was safely on Brunhia. She would miss him, too, but the way he spoke about his new wife told Faith that he needed to be home.

Marcus's wife Samantha was going to have a baby. Superbaby, the proud father-to-be called his unborn child. They were in good hands, the best, and he did not doubt that they were safe. But they were his, and he needed to be with them.

As Faith was thinking about her brother, he joined her on the deck. He sat in the chair beside hers and tried a comforting smile. "You all right?" he asked.

She shook her head. "Not really."

"Hungry?"

"No." Though she had been ravenous lately. And her appetite had never been what one would call dainty.

"You sure you're okay?" he asked again, sounding skeptical.

Faith just nodded. No good would come of opening her heart, no matter how much she longed to do just that.

Marcus didn't press for more, the way Jake would have. He didn't need to. They sat in comfortable silence for a while, admiring the waves and the sun. After a few minutes, he said, "You miss that guy, don't you?"

Faith nodded her head, and tears stung her eyes. Marcus assured her that Luke and Abby were safe. As long as she didn't have any direct contact with them, as long as she stayed far away, they'd be safe. Someone would be watching the people she loved at all times. Nash and Janine, Luke and Abby. All she had to do was stay out of their lives.

In the past nine days, she'd told Marcus a little bit about Luke. But she hadn't told him everything. She hadn't told anyone everything.

If she could open her heart to anyone, it would be Marcus. Maybe that was what family was for.

"I never told Luke that I love him," she confessed. "And now it's too late. It's just as well, considering the circumstances, but I feel like a coward."

Marcus didn't respond, but then she hadn't expected him to. No, he didn't know everything, but maybe he'd heard her whispering "I love you" to Luke as she got onto the noisy helicopter that had taken her away from Rockland. She'd found the words too late. She was always too late.

"You're not a coward," Marcus said gently but firmly.

Faith heard a car in the front driveway but thought

nothing of it. People came and went as a matter of course. Bodyguards, Jake, Maisy, a couple of government officials who had insisted on speaking to her before she left the country. Her safe house was a busy place.

One of the conservatively dressed bodyguards who had already become a part of her everyday life opened the sliding glass door and stuck his head out. "You were expecting a delivery?" He directed his question to Marcus.

"Yep," Marcus said. "Bring it on in."

Marcus took Faith's hand and held it. "Do you remember how we used to take care of each other?"

"Yes." It was what she remembered most clearly, her connection with Marcus. She would miss him when he went home and she was on Brunhia, but it would be different this time. She wouldn't forget—she would never forget.

"That's not going to change," he said, squeezing her hand. "Not ever." His smile widened, and he glanced toward the sliding glass door as it opened again. "Come on out, Doc."

Faith jumped to her feet as Luke, carrying Abby in his arms, stepped onto the deck. Her heart hitched, her mouth went dry. She started to smile, but her smile faded quickly and she glared at her brother, who continued to sit with his legs stretched out casually and his head tilted back so his face caught the sun.

"You didn't have him kidnapped, did you?"

"No," Luke answered. He placed Abby on her feet, and the baby toddled directly to Marcus with a huge grin on her face. She showed absolutely no hesitation when he offered her his arms.

As Luke offered Faith his arms.

She didn't ask questions, didn't ask why or when as they embraced. Luke was here, and for the moment that was all that mattered.

Without releasing Luke completely, Faith again glanced at her brother, who held a very delicate-looking Abby on his lap. "What have you done?"

Marcus shrugged. "I made a couple of quick trips to Rockland, just to see how the place was getting along without you. While I was there, I had a word or two with the Doc." He grinned. "And I got to know Abby, here. Can you say Uncle Marcus yet?"

"Arcus!" Abby said happily.

Marcus rose to his feet, Abby captured snugly in his arms. He gave Faith a brotherly wink and flashed that smile she now remembered so well. "Give me a little credit, Faith. Some things you don't have to be a genius to figure out."

Luke took Faith's hand and held on tight as Marcus headed for the house. "I'm going to show Abby the beach." He tossed a glare at Luke. "You two behave until we get back."

Marcus carried Abby into the house, leaving Faith and Luke alone. Quickly, before she could lose her courage, Faith tipped her face up and said, "I love you, Luke. So much."

He smiled and pulled her close, kissed her and said, "I love you, too."

She let the words wash over her. They had a texture, a substance. They warmed her from the inside out. "What are you doing here?" She held on to Luke tightly, afraid he'd disappear if she let him go.

He threaded the fingers of one hand through her hair, as if he were hanging on to her for dear life, too. "Every day that went past without you in it was so damned long. Nothing was right. I was miserable. I told Marcus one particularly bad night that I shouldn't have let you go. And here I am."

"But your practice, your clinic…"

"Dr. White has taken over."

"Really?" She was genuinely surprised. "*John White?*"

Luke gave her a contented smile. "John likes Rockland and wanted to stay awhile longer, and I handed the reins over to him without a second thought. I think Betsy had something to do with the decision. Molly approves."

"But you love Rockland!" she protested.

"I love you more." There was no hesitancy in that statement. Not a hint of indecision. His blue eyes caught and held hers. "Marry me, Faith. Let me stand beside you, no matter what comes. I want to teach you to fish, and dance, and walk in the woods for no reason except that we want to be there."

It was more than she had ever hoped for, a man who loved her and would stand with her, no matter what. "That's hardly fair," she whispered. "I have nothing to teach you."

He ran his finger along her jaw. "You already taught me how to love again."

Faith grasped Luke's shirt and held on tight. Never again would she let him go. "When this is over, we can go back to Rockland," she said. "I'll build a lab there and concentrate on my research, and you can return to your practice."

"Sounds like a good plan," he said with a smile.

"And until then…" Faith whispered

"Until then, we'll be fine," Luke assured her. "More than fine. Marcus tells me there are lots of

places in the world that could use a couple of doctors.'' A sardonic smile flashed across his face. ''He
didn't tell me exactly where, but I figure I'll find out
soon enough. It doesn't matter. Home is wherever you
and Abby are. It didn't take me long after you left
Rockland to figure that one out.''

Faith rose up and kissed him again. ''Did I tell you
that I love you?'' she asked.

''Yes.''

''Let me tell you again, and again, and again….''

She did just that, in between kisses.

Faith turned to look out on the water, and Luke
wrapped his arms around her, pulling her back to his
chest and holding her close. Marcus and Abby walked
on the beach, the large man and the toddler holding
hands, kicking up sand and apparently carrying on a
deep conversation. Faith watched, deeply and completely content even though she had no idea what the
future would bring.

Well, except for one thing.

On the morning after she'd left Rockland, she'd
awakened knowing that something within her had
changed. She'd come awake and been instantly aware
of dramatic changes in her body. In spite of the chaos
that was her life, that had been a happy day. Almost
as happy as this one.

Faith took Luke's hand and guided it to her stomach. She pressed the flat of his palm there, held her
hand over his and closed her eyes.

And she whispered, ''It's a boy.''

*There are more secrets to reveal—
don't miss out!
Coming in February 2004 to
Silhouette Books*

Abandoned at birth, blind genius Connor
Quinn had lived a hard, isolated life, until
beautiful Alyssa Fielding stormed into his
life and forced him to open his heart to
love, and the newfound family that
desperately needed his help...

*BLIND ATTRACTION
By
Myrna Mackenzie*

FAMILY SECRETS: *Five extraordinary
siblings. One dangerous past.
Unlimited potential.*

*And now, for a sneak peek,
just turn the page...*

# One

"You're different, like me," Jake explained to Connor. "And like Gretchen and Marcus and Faith and Gideon."

"How are they different? How are you different?"

"Some say I'm a financial wizard. Gretchen can solve the toughest puzzle. She's a cryptologist. Marcus has extraordinary strength, and Faith is a gifted physician and diagnostician."

"And Gideon, what can he do?"

"He's gifted in the fields of math and technology."

"Excuse me?" Connor's voice felt like it was coming from a long distance away, faint and hollow.

"He's you," Jake said slowly. "They tried again, and they succeeded. Again."

Connor felt like he'd been kicked in the head. With something very hard. He felt pain flash behind his eyes. Dizziness nearly made him bend over, but he forced himself to stay upright. "They wanted someone perfect this time."

"I won't apologize for our father, Henry. Giving a child up because he doesn't meet expectations, even if you provide for that child, is an unforgivable act. But that wasn't Violet. Our mother didn't know. She grieved for you then and right up until her death."

"How do you know? You were a baby like me."

"She mentioned it. She wrote it in her diary."

But she hadn't known what his father had known, that he was imperfect. Would she have grieved if she had? Anger rose up black and heavy within him. "So you've come to me out of…what? Guilt? Curiosity?"

"I won't lie. I have more than one motive in coming to you. For years, with my memory suppressed, I didn't even know my family existed. Now that I do, I want all of us back together. I want to know my brothers and sisters, and I would have fought to find them no matter what. But there's more."

Connor shook his head. "Explain."

"As I said, I'm investigating the World Bank heist. I need help finding the headquarters of the Coalition. I need someone who can help me find Achilles. Gideon."

"I'm not a detective."

"No, you're not. You're better. You're Gideon's brother. You're my triplet. And Gretchen's. But you're also Gideon's genetic twin in many ways. There are things you know about him, things you understand that I don't."

"You expect me to just accept all this, to take you at your word?"

"I don't have the right to expect anything. I'm merely hoping you'll believe me."

He didn't want to, but dread ran deep in him, and Connor realized that he'd always known that there was something unnatural about him. Now he knew why.

"What if I don't help you?"

Jake let out a deep sigh. "Oliver and Agnes want to do more than grow rich and disrupt the world. They want to run it. They'd like nothing better than to be able to decipher our father's notes and figure out how to replicate his experiments, produce more…people like us.''

''Misfits.''

''Perhaps, but very powerful, nonetheless. If these two renegade scientists produce more children of our ilk, they won't have any concerns about ruining the lives of those children, of using them. They agreed with our father that you were not of value. They tried to steal my life and that of my other brothers and sisters. They did steal Gideon's life, and forced him to turn to evil. Because of them, Violet is gone. We have to stop them. You could help do that.''

''I can't make that decision right now. This requires more careful thought.''

''We don't have much time. They know that we're after them, and they're smart. Moreover, they've got Gideon who's beyond smart. You should know.''

Connor grunted. The legs of Jake's chair scraped across the floor. ''May I say hello to your dog?''

''If he'll let you. This is a…a friend, Drifter.''

''I'll let that pass for now. It's better than enemy. But you should know that I'm determined to bring you into the fold and introduce you to the rest of us.''

Connor stood. ''We'll see.'' But he knew that it wouldn't happen. He'd been alone all his life. It was what helped him to function, and it was too late for family now.

He listened as Jake moved through the house, said goodbye to Alyssa at the front door, then left.

She didn't come inside the office. He'd known that she wouldn't. It was for the best. His thoughts wouldn't leave him alone. He'd always known that his blindness separated him from the world in some ways, but the other thing, that had been the real difference.

Now he knew why. He wasn't real. He was a product, an invention, not much different from the products he invented.

And his difference scalded him. It separated him from all that he wanted.

And he did want, he realized now. He wanted Alyssa in his bed…and more. She was a beautiful woman who should have a man to appreciate that beauty, not a man who couldn't even see all that she was.

She wanted children.

What kind of children, what kind of atrocities, might a man like himself produce?

None. It wasn't possible. His very DNA had been contaminated. Blindness could be the least of the traits he might pass on.

His heart was like a dark, cold stone. He had to get out of here. He had to go somewhere and think. Or not think.

Yes, it was best not to think at all.

He sat there for minutes, realizing that he hadn't lost his family. He'd been given away. He had brothers and sisters, all mutations like himself. He wanted to hug the secret to himself, the way he always had.

Please, God, don't let her find out, he thought as he stalked from the room behind Drifter.

He was nearing the door when he heard her and breathed in her scent.

"You're leaving?"

"Yes." He couldn't say more.

"Was that man really your brother, then?"

"I don't know. Probably." He wished his voice didn't sound so angry. It was like a slap, but he couldn't manage to stop. ''Look, I've got things to do. Work. I'll call you.''

''Of course.'' Her voice was small and clipped.

He should stop, turn to her, touch her, hold her, reassure her. At least talk to her.

But his voice and his sanity were trapped inside him somewhere. Or maybe they were lost forever. What was left wasn't of much value to a woman.

He left without saying another word.

Five extraordinary siblings.

One dangerous past.

Unlimited potential.

## If you missed the first riveting stories from Family Secrets, here's a chance to order your copies today!

| | | |
|---|---|---|
| 0-373-61368-7 | ENEMY MIND | |
| | by Maggie Shayne | ___ $4.99 U.S. ___ $5.99 CAN. |
| 0-373-61369-5 | PYRAMID OF LIES | |
| | by Anne Marie Winston | ___ $4.99 U.S. ___ $5.99 CAN. |
| 0-373-61370-9 | THE PLAYER | |
| | by Evelyn Vaughn | ___ $4.99 U.S. ___ $5.99 CAN. |
| 0-373-61371-7 | THE BLUEWATER AFFAIR | |
| | by Cindy Gerard | ___ $4.99 U.S. ___ $5.99 CAN. |
| 0-373-61372-5 | HER BEAUTIFUL ASSASSIN | |
| | by Virginia Kantra | ___ $4.99 U.S. ___ $5.99 CAN. |
| 0-373-61373-3 | A VERDICT OF LOVE | |
| | by Jenna Mills | ___ $4.99 U.S. ___ $5.99 CAN. |
| 0-373-61374-1 | THE BILLIONAIRE DRIFTER | |
| | by Beverly Bird | ___ $4.99 U.S. ___ $5.99 CAN. |
| 0-373-61375-X | FEVER | |
| | by Linda Winstead Jones | ___ $4.99 U.S. ___ $5.99 CAN. |

*(limited quantities available)*

| | |
|---|---|
| TOTAL AMOUNT | $_____ |
| POSTAGE & HANDLING | $_____ |
| ($1.00 for one book; 50¢ for each additional) | |
| APPLICABLE TAXES* | $_____ |
| TOTAL PAYABLE | $_____ |

(Check or money order—please do not send cash)

To order, complete this form and send it, along with a check or money order for the total above, payable to **Family Secrets,** to:

**In the U.S.:** 3010 Walden Avenue, P.O. Box 9077, Buffalo, NY 14269-9077;
**In Canada:** P.O. Box 636, Fort Erie, Ontario L2A 5X3

Name:_____
Address:_____ City:_____
State/Prov.:_____ Zip/Postal Code:_____
Account # (if applicable):_____
075 CSAS

\*New York residents remit applicable sales taxes.
\*Canadian residents remit applicable GST and provincial taxes.

Visit us at www.silhouettefamilysecrets.com                    FSBACK8

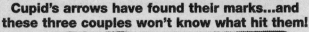

### *Silhouette*®
#### *Where love comes alive*™

FAMILY SECRETS

## Five extraordinary siblings.
## One dangerous past.
## Unlimited potential.

### Collect four (4) original proofs of purchase from the back pages of four (4) Family Secrets titles and receive a specialty themed free gift valued at over $20.00 U.S.!

Just complete the order form and send it, along with four (4) proofs of purchase from four (4) different Family Secrets titles to: Family Secrets, P.O. Box 9047, Buffalo, NY 14269-9047, or P.O. Box 613, Fort Erie, Ontario L2A 5X3.

---

Name (PLEASE PRINT)

Address _____ Apt. #

City _____ State/Prov. _____ Zip/Postal Code

Please specify which themed gift package(s) you would like to receive:

❑ PASSION DT5N

❑ HOME AND FAMILY DT5P

❑ TENDER AND LIGHTHEARTED DT5Q

❑ Have you enclosed your proofs of purchase?

---

FAMILY SECRETS
One Proof Of Purchase FSPOP8R

Remember—for each package selected, you must send four (4) original proofs of purchase. To receive all three (3) gifts, just send in twelve (12) proofs of purchase, one from each of the 12 Family Secrets titles.

Please allow 4-6 weeks for delivery. Shipping and handling included. Offer good only while quantities last. Offer available in Canada and the U.S. only. Request should be received no later than July 31, 2004. Each proof of purchase should be cut out of the back page ad featuring this offer.